The Hand in the Wall

by

–Jean Ann Holland–

Prologue

And it happens again. I uncover a body. It has never been in a basement or attic or even a library. Always in the earth. To me it feels as if the corpse wouldn't have existed if I hadn't been nearby, casually breathing fresh air and soaking in sunshine. Does my presence fabricate tragedy? Am I nature's finder of death? Best I should stay inside. And yet...

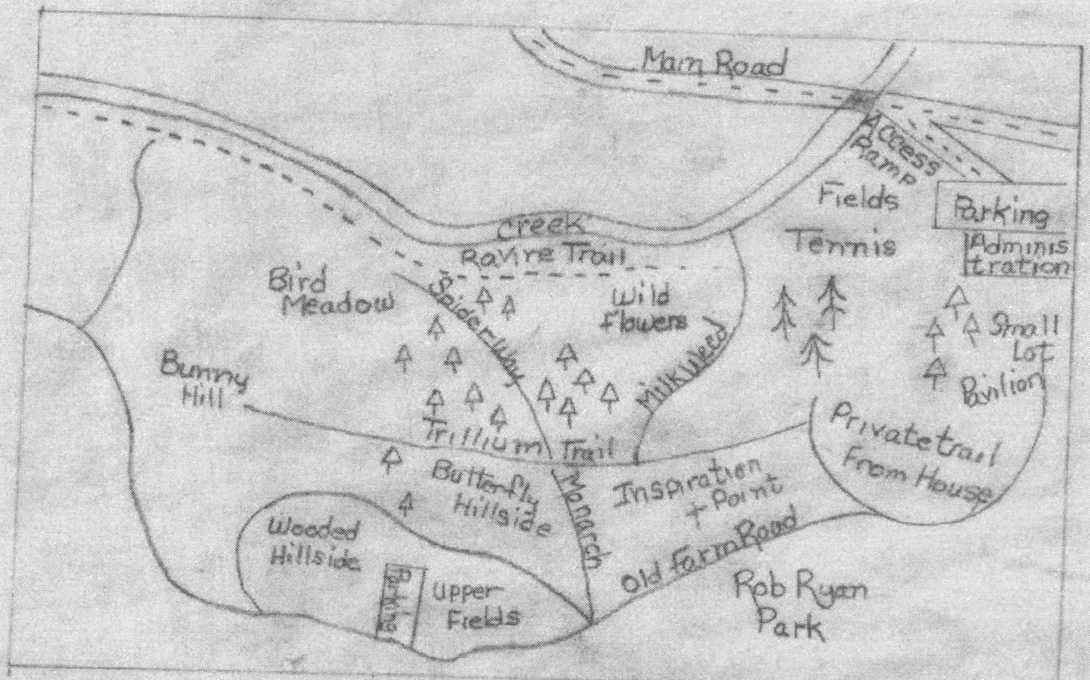
Main Road
Access Ramp
Fields
Parking
Tennis
Adminis tration
Creek
Ravine Trail
Bird Meadow
Spider Way
Wild Flowers
Small Lot
Pavilion
Milkweed
Bunny Hill
Private trail from House
Trillium Trail
Butterfly Hillside
Monarch
Inspiration Point
Wooded Hillside
Old Farm Road
Parking
Upper Fields
Rob Ryan Park

–1–

A gold wedding ring

I am outside in the woods of Rob Ryan Park, as I often am, because there is a force that drives me from my front porch to the four hundred acres of wooded oasis. I am happily traipsing through the forest, drinking in today's sunny skies. I stop and think of past visits. How the change in seasons and wind and sky renews the park on each visit. How in cloudy weather a sense of calm permeates the forest, my footsteps creeping over dirt paths in a gentle rhythm while the occasional bird streaks by, busy with a nest or a worm or whatever birds must rush to. How the wind might tease me and knock my hat to the side which, if I'm lucky and quick, I catch before it hits the forest floor. I laugh at the game we both like to play, the wind and I. And I remember days when it's sunny and the light plays through the leaves and delights me. The glare hits me full in the eye in one spot and shimmers off a pool of water in another. At times it dances, like piano keys playing a complicated air. I take a step and remember that as the light and air change daily, so does the earth beneath my feet. There are days of snow crunching underfoot, leaves crackling to announce my arrival, and soggy loam disfiguring my hiking boots.

I muse about how I have traversed every path here. Some days I start on the path that skirts between the beech trees and, after following a low, trickling stream for a hundred yards, rise to an open field of wildflowers and butterflies. Or, I might trek along an old road, stepping along one of its parallel tracks. But today I walk along the trail that edges the ravine, high above a creek. It is aptly named the Ravine Trail. There is an air of excitement on the trail today because the stream below is running wild. I hear the rushing water. I look down to white water twenty feet below.

The path is narrow, but not intimidating. I've walked here many times. Today it is muddy, mucky even, and I must watch my footing so I don't sink into the spongy soil. And yet it feels serene as birds twitter and a slight breeze moves the dangling leaves overhead. I smile and inhale a deep yoga breath. As I slowly exhale, a squirrel, its tail upright, scoots past me on the left. I reverse my breath, taking a sharp inhale, and step to the right edge of the trail to avoid him. I watch him dodge into the undergrowth. When I move to fully regain the trail, my right foot begins to sink. I lean left to counterbalance, but the soft trail edge gives way, and I find myself sliding downward toward the high, fast flowing creek. "Ooh!" I yell. "Whoa!" I fall on my bottom and slide in the goo. As I am grasping at mud with my hands, my foot hits an exposed root and I am flipped so that now I am sliding on my belly. "Help!" I scream as the sound of the rushing water is getting louder. I make a last grab for a hold and spy something jutting from the wet, moist vertical wall. Straining, I grab on. My hand holds fast and I stop sliding, but now I am dangling over the creek with my belly just grazing the muddy side of the ravine. I kick hard with one foot to hammer the toe of my boot into the bank in front of me. It catches. I look up to see how far I've fallen since it seems a better idea than looking down to see how far the bubbling water is below me. Maybe I can crawl up the side if I ram each foot successively and find higher and higher things to grasp on to. I judge I'm halfway between the path and the water. I look up to see what I can latch onto next. Hopefully it will be less repulsive than the spongy thing I am holding onto now. What is this thing? I squint at it and almost lose my grip at the shock. I am holding onto a human hand! A man's hand wearing a gold wedding ring. It's sticking out of the side of the riverbank. I scream and release my hand from "the hand" in horror and bounce down the slope. I smell the loamy, wet earth. I hear the rushing of water beneath me. And finally, after what seems like forever, I splash into the creek.

~2~

Eerily quiet

The creek is cold and rocky but I manage to keep my head out of the water as I body surf on my back. I'm moving fast. My relief at surviving the fall is replaced by the realization that I need to get off this wild ride. I can see the trees up at the edge of the ravine and they are moving by as if someone pressed fast forward. I call out loudly, "Help!" Again, "Help"! I raise my head and see that I am closing in on a large granite boulder that looks to be about thirty yards ahead. The terror surging through me is only increased by the scrape of a rock on my back or the slap of my hand against a large rock at the water's edge. I squeeze my eyes shut and gulp, afraid to see how close I am to crushing my fragile body on the rock. With a scream I open my eyes to my fate.

There, on top of the boulder, stands a man. I blink. First there was a hand in the bank and now there is a full sized man on a rock. Things are appearing out of nowhere. I try to focus on the man's face as he bends down, extending his hand. I hesitate, narrowing my eyes as I peer at this second hand. But as I come even closer to the boulder, I recover my senses and grab the hand tightly. It is warm and strong.

I step onto the side of the boulder but my boot slips backward into the water. The hand holds tight, suspending me in the air for a second. I pedal my legs and gain purchase on a flat dent in the boulder. Heaving forward and then clamoring upward, I find myself atop the rock. I bend over and rest my hands on my thighs. My hair hangs in wet tendrils over my face. I can see the boots of my rescuer in front of me, so, slowly, I rise up to face him and attempt to scrape muddy water and hair out of my eyes and, with effort, smile. "Thank you," I pant. "I was on a wild ride."

"I saw you," the man says, giving me a sideways stare. "I heard you. You must have fallen in." He backs up a step or two.

"Yes. Slipped right in upstream," I say, breathing heavily. "From the trail. I skirted a squirrel and my foot slipped in the mud and next thing I knew I was falling."

"The trail's high over the creek. Not a good idea to fall that far."

"Well, my fall was broken part way down when I managed to grasp onto, well, I didn't know what it was at the time, but," I pause to think how I should say this, "but I grasped onto a hand sticking out of the side of the bank."

My rescuer grows quiet. After a few seconds he blurts out, "Are you sure?"

"Yes, I am. It was definitely a hand. Sticking out of the muddy hill. It was a man's hand, like yours. In fact, it was about the same size as your hand."

He holds out both hands. "Not mine," he says with a bark of a laugh.

I sit down on the boulder as my legs have become unreliable.

I wipe my hair out of my eyes to better see my rescuer but things are still a bit unclear. "I was so relieved to see you standing on this rock. I don't know what would have happened if you hadn't been there."

He begins to edge backward as if my bad luck might be contagious.

I continue. "We need to call the police. There is a man buried in the hillside, or perhaps just his hand. I'm not sure. I have a phone." I turn to pull my wet phone from my pocket. It was zipped inside so it didn't fall out, but now it is dripping water through my fingers.

"You're okay," I hear my rescuer call as his voice begins to fade. I twist to look behind me and I see that the high banks along the stream have sloped down to level land. In confusion I watch as his back disappears into the woods..

"Wait!" I call at the woods that have swallowed him. "Do you have a phone? What's your name?"

I quickly rise and move off the rock onto land. "We need to call someone," I yell loudly. "About that hand." There is no reply. In fact it is eerily quiet and I can't hear him moving about in the woods. He's vanished.

-3-

Six Pencils

I sit down on the edge of the stream to calm myself. I look at the fast-running water ahead of me and shiver. I remember the hand – how white it was and how cold and mushroom-like. I put my hand in my hair and it comes away full of soppy mud.

"I must have scared him away when I described the hand," I reason. I shiver at the thought of the eerie white fingers. I can still feel the hand in my hand. And who's hand is it? Someone needs to find that out. Determined, I head into the woods. With a solid trail underfoot I feel more like my usual optimistic self.

I zigzag in a general forward direction, hoping I will meet up with someone with a phone or find the park office or a park official or maybe even my car. I have to step over a few strewn rocks and push bright-leaved boughs out of my way. I struggle for half an hour until I see a building sitting up high through the trees. "I think that's the community building," I say to myself. "I'll just cut through the woods and see if someone is there." I look to it as a beacon in the night. I stumble a few times. I have to re-tie my boots once. I finally step onto a parking lot and, slowly crossing the pavement, I find myself on a sidewalk. People are stepping aside to let me by. With a final burst of energy, I pull open the heavy door on the brick building. I step inside.

The large tiled entry is hollow, full of echoes – echoes of boots crossing the open spaces, echoes of doors closing. I shake my head to clear my thoughts. As I scan the area, I see a woman glance up at me from a counter which stands in front of a couple of office doors, one open with a side window, the other solid and closed. The counter itself has a gray laminate top on an imposing red brick base. She is sorting papers that appear to have been shuffled by the wind. There are sheets lying at assorted angles, overlapping and dog-eared. I look closely at the woman and immediately I think of a mourning dove, that small-headed bird with the low coo. As she shifts the papers, she looks up repeatedly, scanning from side to side around the foyer. Her chest is prominent; her dark hair closely cropped. She misses nothing as she orders and reorders papers. She is alert and vigilant. What is she on guard for? As I regard her, she stops and stares at me. Her hands still.

"Who are… what?" She squawks, staring at me.

"I need some help," I blurt out.

"You certainly do. You might start with a bath. And I'd throw those clothes out while you're at it." She rises on her toes and looks down at my feet. "You're making a mess on the floor."

"Well," I say, trying to act calmer than I feel. "I've had a hard day. I fell down into the ravine and took a ride in the creek, but that wasn't the worst of it. During my descent, I was grabbing for something to stop my fall and when I found it, it was a hand. A human hand. Protruding from the side of the ravine."

The woman's face briefly reveals terror. Then she smiles,

holds up finger, turns on her heel and enters the office behind her. I stand waiting, conscious of a few people's stares as they enter the restroom or peruse a framed map of the park. I stare down at my mud soaked boots. After a few minutes the woman returns, giving me a wide berth as she motions me into the small office behind the counter, her papers softly drifting to the floor. She closes the door behind me, firmly.

A middle-aged man in a white shirt motions me to sit in an upholstered chair, but seeing a plain wooden chair on the back wall, I opt for it. His desk is large and holds neat piles of paper. The computer screen is flanked by a colorful notepad and pens angled in a circular metal holder. On the desk lays a lineup of six pencils, sharpened and at the ready. He puts his fingers under the sharp points to align them just so. I can't stop staring at the pencils.

He clears his throat. I look up at him and ask "Are you the park superintendent?"

"No, we don't have that position. I am the Community Recreation Administrator. Margot told me what you said. I'd like to hear it for myself."

I begin at the squirrel knocking me off balance and end at my arrival at his door.

"I think you're lucky you survived the fall and rapid water. That trail is in bad shape, I know. We have had too much rain and the water table is high. And the trail is chopped up. I'll call for someone to close it off." He smiles stiffly. "May I say how sorry I am that you had such a scary fall."

He folds his hands on the desk and gives me a nod. It seems I am being dismissed so I lean forward and utter, "What about the hand I saw in the bank? Don't you think that is unusual and police-worthy?"

Clearing his throat, he straightens his back, readjusts his pencils, and peers at me. "Now, about the hand. You said that you saw a human hand sticking out of the side of the ravine." He pauses. "That's not actually believable. Couldn't it have been an oddly formed mushroom? Or a cluster of roots washed clean by the rain?"

I look him square in the eye and pull my muddy hair from my forehead. "No chance. It was a hand. A man's hand. I have no doubt. It was wearing a wedding ring. You should call the police."

He is about to reply but thinks better of it. He picks up his phone and dials. I can hear the phone ringing on the other end, endlessly. Finally the administrator gives up, emits a long sigh and mutters something about 'have it your way' and picks up a walkie talkie. He barks, "Larry, are you out near the trail? You know, the Ravine Trail that I asked you to close off?"

There is a static reply which the administrator seems to understand. "Good, we have a woman here who claims to have seen a hand protruding out from the side of the ravine. Yes, a hand – human and male." I hear static again. "The trail side, I believe." He looks to me and I nod. "See if you can look over the side and see it." He looks to me again. "Can you describe approximately where on the trail it would be?"

I think. "It's hard to say. A lot has happened since I was hiking up there. But when you mentioned earlier that the ground was choppy, well I remember that it was really choppy where I lost my footing. Maybe that will help."

He nods. He tells Larry and then turns off the radio.

I study him. Then I say, "It might be hard to see it from the top of the trail. I think I was about half way down into the ravine when I grabbed the hand. I think you should get the police on it."

"Well," he says with a half smile. "We try not to bother the police with every little thing we hear from the public. We like to be sure the police need to be involved."

I stare at him in disbelief. I'm being dismissed. The terror of the morning and the tiredness it has evoked decide my next move. "Then I'm going," I state firmly. "I need a bath and I need to rest. Can someone get me to my car? I believe it's on the other side of the park."

Mr. Administrator gives a slight nod. "I'll drive you myself."

And so we silently proceed in his car around the park perimeter. The car is spotless, inside and out. I sit on an old blanket he fished out of the trunk.

"My name is Kate Ranier," I announce, breaking the silence. "In case you have any more questions. I don't have a phone right now. It was a casualty of the swift water. I'll write down my email address in case you or the police want to get in touch with me after the police find the hand."

"Sorry, I should have introduced myself," he replies. "My name is John Logan." He fishes into his breast pocket. "I'll give you a card to keep and one to write your information on."

We take care of formalities when we arrive at my car. My key fob is soaked and emits no signal. I open the slot and pull out the old fashioned key hidden within the fob. "It's gonna cost me to replace this," I think. "And my phone." I watch John driving away. "I doubt I'll get any help from him."

Robert's Story I

Sitting behind the bar on a break, I look around. I am proud and satisfied at how far I have come in two years. I am a partial owner of a new restaurant, yay, and a professional cook, yay, and an important member of a new business. Yay again. After struggling with a brain injury for a number of years and finally taking the time to recover (thanks, Mom... she offered her home as the recovery place) I can say that my life is moving forward. Two years ago, when I was ready to venture out on my own again, I applied for a line cook job at a local restaurant. They knew me. I was a frequent visitor and had talked with most of the staff, especially the bartender Sebastian, and the chef, Bobby. I know my way around food and my insights into the menu made a good impression on Chef Bobby. Good enough that he took a chance on me. Since then I've been working long hours, saving money. And to show for that hard work, I have a car, a new venture on High Street, and an apartment with a fancy balcony where I can put my feet up. Granted, the car is old and the balcony tiny, but they are mine.

And then, a few months ago, the restaurant owners decided to sell out, to retire to somewhere sunny. That was a bad day when I heard that news. But Chef Bobby and Sebastian decided to make a go of it and try to buy the place. They searched around for investors. I had inherited a bit of money and so I bought myself into the venture. It is housed in the same spot where Chef Bobby, Sebastian, and I have been working. I will be a manager/cook and overall fill-in-where-needed partner. Our main investor, Jim Tucci, owns the building. And the place is gorgeous with clean lines and booths with soft seats along the front window. The butter yellow cushions are warm and inviting. And they will compliment the bar. It has a lighted front in yellow and blue. All swirls of color. Behind the bar, rising to the ceiling, are lighted shelves neatly displaying gleaming liquor bottles. Bobby spared no expense on his designer and it was worth it. The colors will show through the front windows and draw people in from the street, especially at night.

Bobby and Sebastian are two creative dudes whose talents were somewhat wasted under old management. They are drunk with excitement to make the new restaurant an upscale bistro. Bobby comes off as a sort of an old-school, bossy chef. But that's a front. His chef's hat is often askew with his brown hair sticking out on all sides. He's stocky and full of energy. And when he gets flustered his cheeks turn bright red. I can see his picture on the front of a series of gourmet frozen entrees. That makes me smile. There is also Jake, Bobby's sous chef, who has taken me under his wing as far as food prep goes. He's fun to hang out with in the kitchen until Bobby starts ranting at him at which point Jake laughs and looks at me over his shoulder, grinning widely, and points to the front of the house. "Out, you pesky man!" Bobby and Jake, what a relationship! Bobby really needs him. Jake is the magic dust on Bobby's dishes. Jake can be somewhat unreliable and Bobby has no time for that. But Jake never takes Bobby's moods and criticism to heart. He is the free spirit of the kitchen.

Sebastian can be found testing out his craft cocktail creations behind the new, sparkling bar. The shining light of this place. He is tall and handsome with dark curly hair. You might call him suave. And funny. His humor is as dry as his martinis. He and Bobby are as different as vodka and rum. But it works. Sebastian keeps the front of the house cool; Bobby keeps the back smokin' hot.

Then there is Jim. Big and bold and brassy, he sashays in, does nothing, and still throws his weight around. He's tolerated because of his investment. Occasionally he has an idea, but mostly he likes to taste food and drink. I'm a bit nervous around him because I'm the new man. Does he think I belong? Bobby believes I have cooking skills and ideas and I do work well with staff. Sebastian appreciates me because I have taken on defining and hiring workers.

And dishes – my task of the hour. While we leased the place with the old fixtures and bought up the barware, we decided the dishes looked like they belonged in a diner. I found a buyer for the lot and am ready to present a new option to Bobby and Sebastian. Bobby's younger brother, Terence, is hauling out the old dishes now and he will take them to another restaurant in the North Hills. I think I've found a great option in dishes – sort of rustic but mainly white to show off Bobby's food. A bit pricer than plain white – which would be fine – but we got a good price on the old ones so why not? At least, that will be my suggestion. Tonight I'm at the restaurant working on the water supply behind the bar. I need to cut in another water line. As I pull up my computer to research how to do this, I hear a deafening crash. That was in the kitchen! I rush back to see Bobby screaming at his brother who is standing amid shards of pottery. The dishes! I wait until Bobby is consolable and put my hand on his shoulder. "We'll re-group," I say. Terrence, the dish dropper, looks to be in tears.

"We were getting money for those so we could buy better dishes. What do we do now?" Bobby screams.

"Chill," I say, "I can rework the plan." In my mind I'm saying goodbye to those nice rustic dishes and hello to the cheaper ones. "Terence, count what we have left and I'll call the other place and see if they still want a partial set." Bobby leaves the kitchen, swinging the door so it crashes into the wall. I get on the phone.

Bobby crashes back in. "Hang on, the dishes can wait. I can't get the backdoor to latch tight. Someone needs to get on it." He scowls at me and then at his brother. 'I'm not sure I can take this. I just wanna cook."

"Temperamental," I think.

"Creative jackass," Terence mutters.

I grab the toolbox and turn toward the door. Terrence has gotten a broom and is ineffectively sweeping up the broken glass.

Sebastian walks in. "Anyone want to try a new drink I made?" He is grinning like a fool and, amid this chaos, he holds a dainty glass in his hand full of pink liquid. Somewhere in his repertoire he has acquired some mini versions of a couple of bar glasses and holds out a small cocktail.

"Go screw yourself," Bobby says and bounds out of the kitchen.

I smile at Terence. "Really, Terence. It's okay. Things happen. Especially in a high tension environment. We all need to calm down." I pat him on the back.

"He treats me like I can't do anything right. In fact, he told me yesterday, 'you can't do anything right.'"

"Ignore him. You're his brother. He feels comfortable taking out his frustration on you. Things will calm down soon."

"What's wrong with the genius?" Sebastian asks, eying the kitchen door which is still swinging back and forth. Then he looks at the floor. "Those are the dishes we sold?"

Terence drops the broom and takes the drink. "Just what I needed," he says with a devilish smile.

I run over, grab the drink from his hand, toss him the broom and say, "Clean up and start counting whole dishes. What a tool you are!" Then I look at Sebastian as I take a long pull on the short cocktail. "You're gonna save us," I announce. And then I head to the back door.

~4~

Deadly Serious

Later that day after a bath and a quick trip to get a new phone, I am cocooning on my front porch wrapped in a fleece blanket because the cool air of autumn is starting to reign. I've been haunted by the hand but have also begun to have doubts as to its existence. Maybe I am crazy. It's been a few hours since I climbed back into my car and left the park, muddied and frustrated. I open my book and look at the words in front of me. They seem to swirl so I shut the book and start for the front door when my phone rings. My new phone.

"Hello?" I ask. I don't recognize the number and wonder if I should have answered.

"Is this Kate Ranier?" a voice responds.

"Who is this?" I reply, warily.

"This is John Logan from Rob Ryan Park. We need you to return here. The police have questions."

"So you found the hand?" I ask, a slight smile crossing my face as I remember John from his office. I am definitely more calm now and can see John sitting stiffly behind his desk.

"Yes." His reply is terse and unrevealing. I almost think I hear a pencil snapping in the background.

"OK. Are the police there? Do they want to talk with me?"

"No, not in my office, but they need to see you in person and would like to walk the scene with you. Can you come to the park … actually, can you go to the spot on the trail where you fell?"

"Sure," I answer brightly. "I want to help."

"How soon can you be here?"

"Forty five minutes," I reply. "I'll meet you all in forty five minutes."

"OK," John says and slams down the phone abruptly.

Thirty five minutes later I am standing atop the ravine, looking down. The trail is impassable as someone has put police tape across it. This is a crime scene now, I realize. I feel a shiver as I remember the fall, the hand, the mud, and the man on the rock. I look down into the ravine. I move my gaze from the rushing water when I hear voices ahead and look up. I see them, a group of seven people moving along the path. They are a somber company, marching in two rows, shoulder to shoulder, barely fitting on the trail – an unexpected sight in my forest. One in the group is John Logan, but then, when I look a bit closer, a smile takes over my face. There, walking toward me, about twenty yards away, but deadly serious and with a commanding manner, is Simone. Simone Serrat, the detective with whom I spent many hours on my front porch. Simone, who confided in me when she was trying to solve a murder in my neighborhood. Simone, who occasionally still pops in to tell me about her latest case. As I watch Simone approach, I see her lean into John Logan as he points at the yellow tape. She is fairly close to me now and, when she turns her head, she recognizes me and says, "Ah no. You aren't involved with this, are you?"

-5-

Hysterical

I walk up to Simone and attempt to give her a hug but she backs off and gives me a nervous look. She is motioning to the team which includes a photographer, John, a tall wiry man, and three men with shovels. Everyone has an appropriately serious face. The photographer is itching his white beard as if to decide if he's ready to take the camera off his shoulder. The shovel men are oddly similar, all a bit short in stature and strong armed with sandy hair. It's like a trio of Lego men from a construction set.

John Logan begins to introduce me but Simone ignores him and addresses me directly. "Tell me what you saw, Kate. Describe in your own words what happened when you discovered the, er, the hand."

I go over the incident of the muddy trail, the sliding, the fast stream, and my locking onto the hand.

"It was lucky that hand was there," I conclude. "It really broke my slide down the side of the ravine and let me get some control of myself. I didn't know what it was until I stopped sliding and looked up, and then I instinctively unclasped it even though I began to descend once more."

"Thank you," Simon says looking at the trail edge. In fact everyone in the small group is gazing there, the shovelers have turned their heads as one.

No one looks at me and I am beginning to feel like a fool. Like someone who comes forth with evidence of a crime but really just wants center stage. But I keep talking because somehow I can't stop myself. "Of course it was horrifying when I finally reached a point of safety and thought about what it meant to have a hand sticking out of a hillside. I couldn't process it until I was safely out of the water."

I look over to see everyone's reaction but they have addressed themselves to their individual missions. The camera is being taken from its case. The shovels have struck dirt.

"OK." Simone breaks the silence and turns her gaze back to me. "You were sliding down the embankment out of control, terrified of the rushing water below, so you grasped for anything to stop your fall. Sounds reasonable. But then," she stops and raises her eyebrows ever so slightly, "you chance upon a hand, a dead hand as it happens, perhaps attached to a dead body buried in the mud of the pathway from which you fell."

I shrug and say, "That's it. But why would someone be buried in the trail, or at least a hand here? It's hard to understand."

Simone turns to the three men who are hard at work. The site has been photographed and everyone not shoveling is watching the dirt as it is turned over. The tall man in the group has a leather bag and stands ready at the edge of the trail – the coroner I think.

"Thanks everyone," Simone says to the group. "I look forward to what you find."

She grasps my elbow and guides me down the path away from the activity.

"Let's go to the car and talk," she suggests.

"OK," I agree. I stop and look over at her. "I don't want to find bodies," I insist. "I just want a calm, happy life with lovely walks in nature and friends and family. Just like anyone."

"I get that," Simone replies in a polite but serious tone. "I also admit this must have been a traumatic experience. Thank you for coming back today and revisiting the scene. Let's talk in the car."

Feeling better, I walk along with Simone until we come to her car, parked near where I left my own. She opens the door for me and gets in the other side.

"I'm glad you weren't hurt," she begins. "But truly, you find two buried bodies within a couple of years." She shakes her head. She pauses. "You know the routine. Is there anything else, anything at all? Of course any detail may be helpful."

I take in a deep breath and remember when this all began. It was a nice walk, albeit a bit muddy, and birds were singing and branches were swaying. I may even have been humming. Not sure. And then the little squirrel scampered onto the trail and my calm was shattered.

"I fell, as you know. I grasped for anything to stop my fall, a root, a branch, anything. But when I grabbed at the only thing I could find, well, it felt weird. It slowed my fall. I was relieved, until I decided to see what I was holding onto. You know, see if it would hold. And there it was, a hand. Definitely a hand." I shiver. "Then I floated madly in the water until I saw a large rock ahead. I thought I would be smashed on the rock. It was horrible." I pause. "But suddenly, as if an apparition, a man appeared on the rock, bent over, and held out his hand. Like an angel in camouflage came down from heaven to pluck me from the water."

Simone gives me a startled look. "Did you hit your head when falling or landing in the water or when you were being washed down the stream?"

"I don't think so. I felt, well, panicked, but not dazed. More clear-headed than one might think."

Simone nods.

"So I grab this proffered live hand and it is strong and is able to pull me out of the rushing water. Enough so I can scramble up the rock. I thank this man, ask him if he has a phone since I am very concerned about the hand in the mud, but when I glance down to show him my ruined phone, he has disappeared."

"What do you mean he disappeared?" Simone is incredulous.

"I know, I get it, but he slipped off into the woods, and try as I might, scanning the woods and calling out, there was no sign of him. Luckily I was able to go through the woods until I saw the administration building. I assume John Logan told you what I told him."

"He did. He gave us his version of the story. He thought you were hysterical."

"Is that the word he used – hysterical?" I demand.

"Actually, yes."

"Well John Logan, Administrator was not exactly a calming influence on a muddy, drippy woman who had fallen twenty or so feet and ridden rapids for some number of yards. He was off-putting and, I would say, cold." I am upset, very upset. It's been a horrible experience and now my sanity is being questioned.

Simone sighs and gives me a vexed look. "It's not in his wheelhouse to deal with crime. Or bodies. He has been very cooperative and, while worried about his park's reputation, quite pleasant."

"Sorry," I say. "I was unsure he would even look very hard for the 'hand' when I left him. I thought he was dismissing me as an unstable person. To use an old-fashioned word – hysterical."

Simone sighs deeply.

"Let's put that word aside. I want to hear more about this 'angel'. The one that magically appeared."

"I wish I could tell you more. He was there in his camo shirt and big boots. And I'm sure I saw a pointy beard. He saved me. Then he disappeared."

"Did he say anything to you?"

"I think he asked if I was OK. He was spare with his words."

"Well, apparently he wanted to get away from you or the situation. But it does seem unusual to rescue some and abandon them in the woods."

"Yeah. That's what I thought. I suppose my talk of a hand in the hillside might have put him off. I mean, of course it would. But, well, I don't know. I guess he was just a man enjoying the woods and, well, perhaps the instinct for flight was too strong."

-6-

More goo

I wait patiently for Simone to comment. Finally she looks up at me with a smile.

I give her a curious look. "You don't think this is amusing, do you? If you had seen me all muddy and making puddles on the Administration building floor, you wouldn't be laughing. The woman behind the counter found me quite inappropriate."

"Of course not. It's just that I got an image of you dripping wet and... it's just so you to stumble and flop in mud. If only I could tell this to my mother. It would make her day."

Simone's mother died a few years before and she still misses her. Her mother was a sounding board for Simone when she was noodling out a crime. In fact, Simone and I are good friends now because my sense of humor and insight into human motivation remind her of her mother. And I think I entertain her with my tendency for pratfalls and self destruction. Ours is an unlikely friendship formed in the tension of unraveling a crime in my neighborhood.

Simone takes my hand. "I'm sorry," she says gently. She looks away for a minute then turns to me, becoming serious again. "Let's get down to it. What did your rescuer look like? Hair color, eye color, distinguishing marks."

"Well, my eyes were blinking back water and mud. I tried to clear them with my hands but that added more goo."

"Again, I find it odd he just walked away like that. You said you asked him if he had a phone?"

"Yes, it was strange. He just melted into the forest. Once he pulled me up on that boulder he wanted nothing else to do with me. Do you think he has anything to do with the dead man?"

"What makes you think it's a man?"

"Hand size."

Simone smiles. "Okay, makes sense. There is no real reason to think he might be involved with the death or burial, but the fact he was in the park and sneaked away is a concern."

She continues. "Anything else you remember about anything—the hand, the man, …?"

"Nope. Do you have any idea how long that body could have been there? I'm assuming it's a whole body."

"I think so, and no, it's a very cold crime scene, not fresh, so you're the best source of information we have at the moment." She smiles at me. "Again, you are our best witness." She gives me a quick hug. "I worry about you. Your propensity for stumbling upon crime." She smiles at me. A warm, caring smile. The most human reaction I've had since this whole ordeal began. "You can go home now. Rest. Have tea. I'll be in touch."

"Ok. Anything else I can do to help?"

"I'm okay on my own. But I'll be by later to see how you are and ask more questions."

"I feel better already. See you soon. I'll make you tea." With a wave, I get into my own car to head home. As I draw the seat belt forward, I feel very tired. I look back towards Simone's car and she is standing there, smiling at me.

-7-

Sing it again

It's the next day and the morning is crisp. I stretch out on my porch swing to continue waking up. I sway back and forth with air lightly moving over my face. A bird belts out an exuberant song. Dreamily I continue my motion – back and forth. "Sing it again, birdie, sing it again," I mumble. And then the next thing I know I am laying on a still swing with the sun in my face.

"What time is it?" I ask myself, looking down at my watch. "Oh, crap, it's nine already. That bird sang me a lullaby." I rise from the swing and go inside to the kitchen and press the button for an espresso. I hear the grinding of the machine as I move back through the living room, grabbing my computer on the way. Plopping down on the sofa, I pull up the Post Gazette. I check out each page perfunctorily. "Not much going on here," I think. I remember the coffee so I dash back into the kitchen and carefully bring the small cup and saucer back with me to the living room. After a sip, I address the electronic paper again.

After a few clicks, I come upon the obituaries. Death notices have always held my interest. The ages of people, the kind words, the requests for donations. A life can be gleaned in only a few sentences.

Methodically moving down the page, I glance at each notice. Most have lived long lives and left family behind. Sometimes the photo is an old one, the ninety year old looking like their thirty year old self again. It's nice. It gives them more personality. I continue to scan through the names and pictures until I come to a photo of a handsome, healthy looking man with a lot of white hair. My eye catches the ending where it says 'donations can be made to the Western Pennsylvania Naturalists Club.' That's a nice gesture, I think. I hope they get a lot of donations. I back up and read the obituary from the top. 'Derek Remy of Pine Township died suddenly sometime last week. He is survived by his brother, Dale Remy. There will be a memorial on Wednesday, Oct 12, at the Moonstone Country Club between 7 – 9 pm.'

Moonstone Country Club, I ponder. I don't know that one. And what is that about 'died sometime last week'? That's odd. I re-read the entire notice. It goes on about Derek Remy's devotion to natural areas and his successful career in technology. It says his wife preceded him in death. That's sad. He's only 55 and she is gone as well. I look up from the computer, thinking. Through the back door, I notice a bird hop onto the patio table. And just then a thought pops into my head. Oh, the poor man's body wasn't discovered right away and time of death is very sketchy. Sudden – unwitnessed accident? Major health event with no one around to help? Foul play?

And then I have it. This is the man whose hand I grasped Rob Ryan woods. He was buried in the wet mud for an undetermined amount of time and it is unclear exactly when he died. I put down my computer and think about the hand I grasped. It's owner may have been in the woods hiking when the tragedy happened. A fall perhaps. I think about hiking alone on a trail and what might happen if you had a bad fall. But how did he become buried under the trail?

Is Derek Remy truly the man in the trail? I need to talk with Simone.

~8~

How long have these been on the store shelf

"Simone," I speak into the phone. "I haven't seen you since, well, since the... the.. woods, um, yesterday. Stop by for some tea."

"Okay, you sound upbeat. What's going on?"

"Not much. I hope things are going well on the case that I uncovered."

"Early days as you know. Please don't ask me for information that is not yet public."

"I won't. I just want to check with you on something I may have figured out."

"About what?"

"C'mon. Come have some tea. I'll find a couple of cookies too."

"If I weren't driving down 910 at this very moment, I wouldn't do this, but okay, I'll be over."

"Perfect," I say. "Stop at the Superette and get some cookies, will you?" I hang up.

I put on the tea kettle and drop a couple of teabags into

cups. As the water begins to boil, I hear Simone pull into the driveway. I fill the cups and then let her in. She hands me a bag of Oreos.

"So what's up?" she asks, dropping into a chair. "I hope you have figured out that you should stay away from that crime scene?" She gives me a knowing look. "Don't get involved in this one. Didn't happen in your neighborhood. Just unfortunate you were in the wrong place at the wrong time."

I take a deep breath and wrap my hands around the warm mug. "Today I read an obituary for a Derek Remy. I think you know the name."

"What did it say?" she replies.

"His date of death is unclear and he was a naturalist. A possible sudden death in the woods? At least that's what came to me when I read about his life and death."

"You are drawing a conclusion from very little evidence. But, okay, no harm in telling you that you are right, this time," she gives me hard look, "but that's all you need to know. Pass the cookies."

"Oh come on. Tell me more. I discovered the body. You know I can be discrete. And I was a big help in that death over there." I point through the window and across the street as I plow ahead. "I read he has a brother – only next of kin. Did he have to identify the body?"

Simone sighs and I know she will tell me more. I am a sounding board for her.

"Yes. He drove in from somewhere around Chicago. Then he had to identify the body which is always an ordeal. Looked rumpled, not well kept but he had driven quite a few hours."

"Why comment on his appearance? Doesn't seem your style."

"Well, a detective notices things because they give you hints about a person. The first thing that popped into my mind was that it could be a case of perfect brother and loser brother, if you'll excuse my crude assessment. And everything I've heard about Derek or the photos I've seen of him show him to be well dressed and wealthy looking. Anyway, just a theory that occurred to me. Probably should ignore it but, well, instincts." She shrugs.

"So Derek was perfect brother. And loser brother, what's his name – Dale – will inherit?"

"As I said, only a gut reaction. Not sure of much yet. Just gathering information about the people surrounding Derek's life. A children's school – a charity of Derek's wife – has a claim, maybe, at least possibly, on some money. Still clearing that up."

"So, was Derek well-liked?"

Simone hands me a cookie. "No more questions. But I congratulate you on figuring out that Derek Remy was the body in the park." She leans back and takes a sip of tea. "Aah," she exhales. "Always calms me."

"See, that's the idea. You come here, we talk, you relax, I find insight into your latest investigation, we..."

"Hey," she says, ignoring my musings. "Pull up the obit for me, will you? I haven't seen it."

I oblige and watch her eyes move back and forth on the illuminated screen. "The memorial is already scheduled, huh? Dale is an efficient man."

Simone snaps the laptop shut and puts down her tea. She

looks around the room and out the window, then bends her arms over her head, relaxing into the chair. "How's Robert? Still in the restaurant business?"

"You know he is. Haven't you popped in yet?"

"No, I'm working and Robert and crew are all hard at work too. How's he managing head-wise? I would think it would be stressful to open a new place. As you know, I also experienced a brain trauma like Robert so I know these things."

"Oh, don't I know. You and Robert, TBI this and TBI that. Not to make light of it though." I give an apologetic smile and settle back. "Robert seems totally happy. Very upbeat. And he has great confidence in the chef and bartender. They all put in some money and they rounded up an investor. Robert will be a cook/manager of sorts. At first anyway. He has talents in the food creation arena, at least I think he does. Self taught, resourceful. So it all seems good. I'll have to tell him that I found another body, or hand."

"He finds your amateur sleuthing to be unnerving."

"Yes, but I can't be secretive. It will come out. He'll want to know everything."

"Please don't drag him into this. When he lived here the whole murder thing with you as a suspect made him very, very nervous. Let him enjoy himself. A new business. What more could a young man want?"

"I'll try, but I'm focused on this experience in the park. Can't help it," I respond.

Simone rises. "You're hopeless. And I've got to go. I'm busy. Too busy for this tea and these lousy cookies. How long have these been on the store shelf?" She looks disparagingly at a cookie and announces, "And, once more, my advice to you is to keep your sleuthing to a manor house in the English country-side. You know," she smiles, "focus on a book."

She sets her mug into the kitchen sink, puts a whole Oreo in her mouth, and waves goodbye. Boy, when she decides to exit she doesn't waste time. I dunk a cookie and watch her car pull away. I guess I have to savor the short visits.

—9—

General wonderfulness

Later I decide to Google Derek to find out more about him. There is no humanity in being a dead hand in a muddy hillside. He deserves more. I need to get to know more about the living man. In the search results I come upon a different obituary for him. The photo is in color and wording is longer, much more complete. Wow, the accolades! This more complete notice is full of stories of his charity work, his commitment to the environment, his general wonderfulness. "How did he end up where he did?" I wonder. "A body under a path." I stare at the photo. He surely was a handsome man with blue eyes and white thick hair. I click on more pages from Derek's search. Oh my. He was a large contributor to Rob Ryan Park! I shiver. To think he was found under a trail in that same park.

I click on another link. Another Remy obituary appears but this one is of his wife Rhonda, missing and presumed dead after an ocean swim off the coast of New Jersey. Wow, I say to myself not for the first time during this Google search. That's sad. She was never found. Was he despondent? Oh, but it wasn't a suicide. He couldn't have buried himself. Was he implicated in the death and there is a grudge from someone in her family? But the obit says nothing about her family at all.

I click on a few more pages where he is mentioned. I should probably stop snooping around his life, but I want to know. I keep thinking about the poor man and about his lost wife. And yet, Derek was far from poor. I know this because I just read on another web page that he had sold his tech company for millions.

As I shut my laptop I scold myself that I should mind my own business. But I know I won't. I think I'll spend some time in the park he so loved and supported. Maybe I can get a better picture of him. The people in the offices at the administration center may have known him since he was a benefactor of the park. I could try to talk to that couple I keep offending – John and his assistant. Tomorrow I will plan my investigation at the park. Simone never needs to know until I uncover the pivotal clue. I draw my face into a big, goofy smile.

~10~

Self-talking

It's the next evening and I decide, with much bolstering of courage, to stop by the open house memorial for Derek. I can't get the memory of the hand in the hillside out of my mind. If it weren't for me, the body may never have been found. Maybe. It makes me feel a closeness to Derek. My plan is to start my investigation at the park tomorrow.

When I walk into the facility, I see what must be Derek's brother shaking hands in front of a picture of Derek. He favors Derek. A little chubby and I can see the disheveled bit. I stand in the line formed to greet him and pay respects. I wait nervously and chant to myself, "So sorry for your loss. I was an acquaintance of Derek's and he was very helpful to me. I want to pay my respects." I have rehearsed these lines. They are absolutely true – I am sorry Derek's body was buried in the woods especially since I had to be the one to find it when I "met" him last week, and since he may have saved my life with his dead hand, he was extremely helpful. I will be brief, say only the prepared lines, and then leave. It's all about closure, I think.

When it's my turn to greet Dale, I freeze. He holds out his hand. He gives me a welcoming smile. He has kind eyes, blue like his brother's. I begin to feel more at ease and I grasp his fingers.

"Uh," I begin, "Um, I'm sorry about your brother."

"How did you know him?" he asks perfunctorily but never dropping his eyes from mine.

"I, um, met him at the park … where he was unfortunately found." (Ugh.) "He was a great help to me."

"How so?" Dale inquires.

"Well, he was very nice to me. He…" I drop my gaze for a minutes. I feel like a fraud. After a couple of seconds I look up into Dale's piercing blue eyes. They twinkle and have creases around the edges.

"He helped me once when I had a fall in the park."

"That's a kind story. Thank you." Derek's brother gives me a weak smile. I know I am now dismissed but I can't seem to walk away.

"He gave me a helping hand," I ramble, "when I slipped. His hand was strong and stopped me from a bad fall."

"Wait," Dale insists, now grabbing my hand. "Are you the woman who found his body? The one who noticed his hand protruding from the bank?"

I mumble and turn to leave but he squeezes my fingers. "It's okay," he blurts. "It must have been awful for you."

"I'm sorry," I mutter. "I shouldn't be here."

"Really, it's okay. It must have taken guts to come here tonight and I can see how finding a body would give one a connection to it. And to his family."

I glance over to the photo of Derek.

"And how hard for you!" I exclaim. "To lose a brother."

"Thank you," says Dale, still focusing his gaze on me. "We had a, um, complicated relationship."

He looks down. Not sure if he is sad that Derek is gone or sad about their relationship.

But now, I feel overwhelmingly sad. "Well, I will be going now."

"Oh, thanks and, um, you are?"

"Kate Ranier."

"I saw your name in the police report!"

What was I thinking? Coming here, bothering this grieving man.. I smile, shrug, and hope my appearance wasn't too upsetting to Dale.

~11~

My God, be careful

W hen I get home, I decide to run down to the Chinese takeout. After I place my order, I look down the street and the lights are on in Robert's restaurant. I meander over.

"Robert," I call gaily as I see him ducking behind the bar. "How are things? I'm just waiting for my Shrimp in Garlic Sauce and I saw the lights on here."

"Yup, still fussing around. How did this bar area get a mess with no one even ordering drinks?" He looks at me in exasperation. "I'm afraid I'll be running around tidying all the time." He takes a deep breath. "I haven't seen you in a bit. How are you?"

I pause. Robert will be very unsettled when I tell him about the body and about Derek Remy. But he will have to know.

"Have a seat my dear," I say, pointing to a chair. "I have some news."

"News, huh? Okay. Shoot."

"Well, a couple of days ago I was hiking at Rob Ryan, which I know is a favorite haunt of yours." I pause. He just keeps looking at me in anticipation.

"So, something really odd happened. I was on the Ravine Trail, you know, above the creek?"

Robert nods.

"And, well, the creek was high and fast and the trail was soggy. I mean really deep, gooey mud. And, anyway, my foot sank in at the edge of the trail and I sort of fell down the embankment."

"Oh! How far did you fall? That's pretty high up there."

"Um, well, all the way to the creek."

"What? You landed in the water? How are you not hurt? My God, be careful Mom." He puts his hand to his forehead. "How did you get out of there? Did you crawl back up?"

"No. Here's the whole story."

Robert gives me a look and settles back into his chair. "I'm ready… I guess."

"So," I continue, "as I said, my foot sort of turned in the goo and I found myself over the edge, heading downward. I grasped at the hillside to find something to hold to, and I did. And it stopped my fall."

"Well that was good. That probably saved you from injury."

"Yeah, it did. But the thing is, while it stopped me for a bit and slowed me down, when I examined what I was holding onto, I found it was a human hand. And, so, obviously I released my grip and then continued into the creek. But I'm okay." I extend my arms to show I am still in one piece.

"A human hand! What do you mean you grabbed a human hand?"

"It was jutting out of the side of the ravine wall. It was awful."

"Whose hand?"

"His name is Derek Remy. He was buried in the trail."

Robert says nothing. I can see him digesting this information. And I can see it's not going well. How could it?

"Some poor guy was buried in a trail in the park? How... who...?" He has lost his words.

"Simone is working on that."

"But you found him?"

"Yes, I did. And I reported him to the park office people who called the police. By the way have you ever met those people in the Administrative building?"

"No, never met them. You walked in with a tale about a hand in the bank and then..."

Robert trails off. Maybe I should have prepared him more for this story. He is stunned.

"OK, Mom. That must have been a terrible experience for you. I'm sorry you had to deal with it. But, at least you got the police – Simone, wow – and did what was right. Are you okay?"

"Yep, I have gotten used to it. I even met Derek's brother at a memorial service today."

"Wait." Robert stands and begins to pace. "So since I last saw you, you have fallen into the creek, grabbing a dead hand on the way down. Reported it to the police and," he stops and stares at me, "gone to a memorial service for the owner of the hand?"

"Well I was curious."

"And what did you learn?" Robert now leans in to me, his eyes large.

"That Derek appeared to be a very nice man who was a big contributor to the park and, well, that's about it. Oh, and his wife died a year or so ago. She drowned."

"In the creek?"

"No, no. In the ocean. Oh, and his brother was at the memorial and seemed very nice."

"Have you spoken to Simone?"

"Oh, yes. I have been debriefed."

"And what did she say about you finding a body… another body?"

"She was surprised. As was I. I didn't like it."

"OK. I might give her a call."

"Go ahead. Good idea. She can verify that I'm not crazy."

Robert returns to his seat. He grabs my hands and smiles at me. "I'm so glad you're okay. It sounds like a dangerous fall. But wait, you said you went into the creek. How did you survive that and get out of the water?"

Just then the door opens and the lovely woman from the Chinese restaurant comes in with my dinner. I thank her and turn back to Robert.

"I was lucky. I landed safely in the water without hurting myself and sort of back surfed down stream and then, just as I was about to hit a rock, a man appeared to pull me out. Really, I was quite lucky."

"Who was the man? I'd like to thank him."

"That's just it. He turned and left me on the rock and disappeared into the woods."

"He climbed up the embankment and left you there?"

"Oh, no. At this point in the creek the ravine had ended and the water was level with a path into the woods. So, I bushwhacked my way through the woods and found the administration building. You're sure you haven't dealt with those people in there?"

"No. Didn't really know there were 'people in there.'"

"Okay, well I'm off to eat my dinner."

"Just like that? You leave me with this tale and take off?"

Frankly, I can't wait to escape his incredulous but somewhat accusing look. I fiddle with the plastic bag I'm holding. I need to go. I feel so bad I've dropped this on him but I have a strong flight instinct welling up inside me. "Call Simone. She'll fill you in."

Robert's Story II

So tonight, Mom comes into the bistro, happy and smiling, waiting for her dinner from the take out place a few doors up. Then she proceeds to relate a horrible tale of how she almost fell to her death and oh, by the way (as she tells it) discovers a dead hand in the middle of her fall. I'm not kidding. She lays this on me while waiting for Chinese food. As soon as I'm done here I have to call Simone and see if Mom is losing her mind.

Then, as she is leaving the cafe, Mom runs into Sebastian. Of course he feels bad because he almost knocked her down, but she finds it amusing.

"You guys are scurrying around here, aren't you? Much to do!" Mom chirps.

"I'm sorry. My mother told me that there is always time to be polite." Sebastian is embarrassed.

"Aw. I'd like to meet her. Will she be in here sometime do you think?"

"She'll be here for the opening. She already put in her drink request."

"I'll join her then," Mom says with a big smile. She conducts this little conversation as if she has not told me a story that has me reeling.

So then, Sebastian spies me standing behind the bar. "What

are you doing back there?" he says sharply, his manner switching from ingratiating to accusatory in a flash.

"Me?" I ask, pointing my thumb to my chest.

"Bottles are missing," Sebastian calls out. "I'm not accusing you Robert but there is a least a case of some very good bourbon missing...vanished."

"I was just straightening up. I know this is your territory but things were quite, er, messy. Out of alignment."

"Yes, 'cause I was trying to find the bottles."

"Oh, I get it. But I didn't see any bourbon stashed away."

Mom pipes in. "Is the door open to the public? I think I've sashayed in on occasion and the door wasn't locked so, I guess anyone could have..."

"Only when we are going in and out with stuff." Sebastian interrupts. "We're pretty careful."

"Maybe Bobby needed it for something," I guess. "No, that doesn't make sense, how about Jim? He tends to think he owns the place."

"Well he owns part of it," Sebastian admits. "But not enough to abscond with stock. Not sure how to approach this." He walks into the back room in disgust.

Mom gives me a little wave. "I'm off. Sorry about that theft. Be sure to lock this behind me," she advises.

I stare at her, not sure how to react to the sequence of story about death-chirping to Sebastian-waving to me. Walking to the door, I shake my head and I wave back. No sooner have I turned the lock than Terrence knocks on the glass. I open the door to him.

"Careful, Sebastian is upset because bourbon is missing.

You don't know anything about that, do you?" I give him a once over.

"No," Terrence says, insulted by my question.

He stumbles as he comes through the doorway. I look at his feet. He has on big, red sneakers. "No wonder you tripped," I point out. "Those shoes are too big for you. Where did you get them?"

"Oh, just at a store."

"Didn't they have your size?"

"They fit fine. I tripped because you didn't open the door wide enough and I caught the toe. Are you afraid a thief will slip in?" He guffaws. "Maybe we need a big dog."

"What're you doing here?" I wonder aloud.

"Bobby asked me to stop by. Is he in the back?"

"Yep."

"I'll go back there then," he says, turning on his heel.

"You'd be better received if you walked in with a case of bourbon."

Terrence ignores me and walks on.

So that was my evening in the bistro. I may hide away on my balcony tomorrow.

~12~

He was no friend of mine

I have an hour or so until dark and I can reheat this food. Because I can't stop thinking about Dale and Derek, I am compelled back to the park. I return to the woods with an overwhelming need to meander back along the Ravine Trail. I arrive at the spot of my accident, and skirt around the police tape. The problem with being a witness in a crime is that you feel you have special privileges, you are part of the police crime team. I hope they aren't monitoring footprints because mine will be everywhere. But now that the body is gone, what is the harm? I look at the trail and it's still mucky. I look back at the yellow police tape. Is this still here for safety or because it's considered an active crime scene?

I look further down the trail. It's shadowy and hard to see, but I discern a tall man standing within the tape. I'm not the only interloper. Suppose it's a friend of Derek's! How sad. How touching. Seeing where his good friend last lay. I approach quietly. I don't want to interfere with his moment, but, despite my misgivings, I allow myself to edge toward him. As I do, I see him spit on the dirt. The dirt under which his friend lay dead! I stop. Dear friend of Derek's? Perhaps not. Maybe this is the man who killed him and buried him, coming back to the scene. The man sees me and looks up. "Come on," he says. "I don't care if you trample this ground."

"I think the concern may be safety," I mutter, but loud enough for him to hear. When I reach him I hold out my hand and say, "Hi. I'm Kate. I was hiking here and fell and found your, er, friend's body quite by accident. It was me who reported it."

"My friend!" the man chokes. His face reddens. "He was no friend of mine. He killed my sister. He killed her and didn't even give us a chance to say goodbye. Just lost her at sea. Drowned her." He spits again. I look down to see phlegm in the muck. I slowly raise my eyes and stare at him.

He kicks at the ground and I take his arm and say, "That's not what happened. No one said he drowned her. She was swimming too far from the shore and was lost in a current, a rip current, or something that she could not overcome. That's what I read."

"What do you know? Derek wanted her gone. He had found someone else and she was in the way!"

I'm taken aback. "I, er, I ..." I trail off. For once I am speechless. I try again. "I thought he was devoted to her and mourned her terribly. I'm sorry. I just..."

The tall, lean man seems to take me in again. He sighs. "Derek was a player. Good looking, rich, beloved by some. Even I liked him when he was my brother-in-law. But after Rhonda disappeared, I came to my senses. She had just promised a lot of her earnings to a children's experimental school and he hated that. I don't know why. Rhonda was so devoted to it. Rhonda said he seemed suspicious of what he called 'that woman from the school' but Rhonda was no sucker. It would have made her so happy in those last days of her life had he come on board with the school." Rhonda's brother stamps his foot. He smiles at me. "I'm glad he's gone. And on this godforsaken muddy, butt-ugly trail."

"Oh, I love this trail. It's not ugly. It's..."

He pivots to put his back to me. But as he does, the goo snags a foot and, before he can right himself, he begins to slide. He grasps the police tape but just pulls it all with him as he starts to disappear over the edge of the ravine. I'm paralyzed. His lower body disappears and then his shoulders and then all I can see his hand, reaching up for a grasp. I lunge for him and tightly hold onto his hand. He's much heavier than me and his hand is a bit muddy but somehow, by laying on my stomach and holding his hand with my two hands, he manages to regain the trail. We both lay in the mud, breathing hard. I turn on my side to look at him. He's staring up through the treetops. They are swaying a bit and that movement seems to calm him.

As he sits up he starts to yell, "That bastard! He almost got me.'

He gives me a quick glance and returns to staring at the sky above. I sit up and my movement seems to rouse him. He turns his face to me and looks up. He's handsome but now his lovely blond hair is full of mud. He gives a hard smile and says, "Thank you for helping me. But let me warn you. His spirit is back here and seeking revenge. If I were you, I would stay as far away from this park as I could."

He stands, holds out a hand to help me to my feet, salutes me, and troops off. I want to sit down and go over what he's said.

His description of Derek seems so far off from what I've read. But I was reading an obit so… I look down to find a comfy spot to sit and reflect but soon realize it's quickly becoming dark. I wander to the car, my final steps stumbling in the dark.

~13~

Devotees of the woods

The next day as I lay in bed, seeing the sun cast shadows through the window, I think about the Ravine Trail and my encounter with Rhonda's angry brother. And still I am drawn to the trail. I tell myself there may be clues there or suspicious people milling about. I can be eyes and ears in the park for Simone. I'm certainly not going to find clues in my house and I want to know what happened to that man I found. I close my eyes and picture myself wandering along the path. I shake my head to change the image. Do I really think I can be of help meandering around the park or has the park become a compulsion? Raising on my elbows in bed, I listen to a bird outside the window. The day is lovely and I want to be out in it. Just the sort of day I like for walking or hiking. I think about the park, about the tragedy there, and conclude I will enjoy that park as I always have – roaming over trails and listening for critters and enjoying the quiet and peace that it brings me.

When I step from the car, I decide to take the Trillium Trail because my head says not to retrace my steps on the Ravine Trail. The Trillium Trail crosses the Monarch Trail which leads to the largest meadow in the park. The Trillium Trail is loaded with leaves – some bright yellow, some dark, mottled red, and some plain brown. My boots are crunching them with each step. I negotiate my way to the cross path of Spider Way. Really, who named this trail? I turn onto it despite the fact that it will lead over to the Ravine Trail. My head has lost to my heart. I shouldn't go there but I think of the hand, Derek's hand, and I want to have a silent vigil there for a few moments. I am going in the reverse direction from the day I made my clumsy but spectacular fall into the stream. Now the ravine will be on my left. I stumble along Spider Way, reviewing my treacherous fall. I stop and sigh. I need to change my thoughts. I look ahead. There is a lovely honey locust ahead whose leaves are bright yellow. They flutter gracefully to the ground. I look up into the branches when I arrive at the tree. This is why I always came here – to stand alone in the quiet and let a leaf tumble onto my face. The wind is gentle so the leaves drop like light tears. When I come to the junction with Ravine Trail, I turn right. It's still soggy so I proceed very carefully and not at all close to the edge. After two or three minutes I come to the spot where I had my fall and notice lots of footprints – me and Rhonda's brother and two, even elongated rectangles where we lay on the ground. I peer over the edge of the trail and see the yellow tape hanging over the stream. And down below, walking along the fast stream, barely maintaining his footing on the narrow edge, is my rescuer in camouflage. I think of waving or calling out to him, but he is intent on his movement and wouldn't hear me over the rush of water. I watch him for a couple of seconds before turning my attention to the trail. Rambling on, I consider Derek, who in his death may have saved my life. I find myself on a trail with no name marker. The administration building lies ahead. I can see it sitting up in the distance. It seems all paths lead there. Well, I conclude, that makes sense. I suppose it is the center of the place.

As I go up the gentle slope to the center, I spy Simone in the parking lot. "Oh man," I think. "Why does she have to be where I am?" I need to avoid her as she is, I'm sure, on official business. Too many people around here know my role in the incident. I enter by a different door and find myself standing outside a small cafe. "Huh?" I huff, "I didn't know there was a cafe here. I've only used the other door for the bathroom and, well, to report the hand." I slip into the cafe and sit down, easily avoiding Simone who probably went into the door by the offices and bathrooms. As I gaze up at the menu on the wall behind the cafe counter, a smiling young woman asks me what I would like.

"Tea, I say. Maybe mint. Yes, mint," I decide. I sit down at a little bistro-type table that overlooks the woods. "Well, it's very nice," I think to myself. "How did I not know this was here?"

And then Simone is standing next to my table.

"What are you doing here?" she demands. "I would have thought this was the last place you would go."

"Would you like to join me?" I say with a graceful gesture toward the other chair. "I'm having tea."

Simone begins to say something but just then the woman I remember from outside the administrator's office, Margot I believe, calls into the cafe. "Larry Cloud is in John's office. You can go in now."

"Larry Cloud?" I inquire.

"Yes. I have an appointment. Enjoy your tea," Simone says, rising and casting a quick, terse smile in my direction.

"Larry Cloud?" I ponder. "I wonder who that is?"

My tea arrives, steaming and very minty. I comment to the cafe attendant, "I have been hiking here for a few years and never knew about the cafe. Is it new?"

She replies, "Yep. It was really Derek and Rhonda Remy's idea to have a cafe here. Derek used to invite his friends from the nature organizations here. They were all devotees of the woods and the whole park, really. I miss Derek. He met with an accident and he died recently. Tragic. His body was found here in the park."

She pauses and then smiles at me. "Enjoy your tea."

The cloud of steam above my teacup reminds me of the name I just heard - Larry Cloud. I wonder who it is. I assume he is a person of interest… No that's too strong. Someone that may know something about the park or the path or … My mouth opens in a big O. "Oh," I infer, "The Larry that was called on the radio gadget by John when I was sitting in his office all muddied up. The guy who went to the trail to try to find the hand. No wonder Simone is meeting with him. Man, I'd like to be a fly on the wall or a little mouse in the corner when that talk happens."

I grab my tea and head down the hall to the open area outside the office. I can't see Simone anywhere. She's probably behind closed doors with this Larry Cloud fellow.

"Hey," someone calls. "What are you doing here?"

Turning my head, I see none other than the scowling Margot.

"Oh hi. Margot, right? I'm Kate and since we seem to be bumping into each other..."

"Margot, yeah" she replies flatly.

"I just picked up tea at the cafe. Very nice feature."

I hold the steaming cup up in front of me. "Could I get you something? I always seem to be bugging you."

My openness works. Margot smiles.

"No, thank you. You seem put together today."

"Yes, I've had a few bad days, I admit."

My hand is getting hot from being wrapped around the tea-cup and I sit it on her counter. She gives it a dark look.

"Oh, sorry." I reach for the cup. It falls onto its side. The tea floods some papers on the counter and then drips on the floor in front of Margot. She follows the tea's path with angry eyes.

"Let me get paper towels," I call as I head to the bathroom. When I return, laden with a thick brown pad of them, I find her grabbing papers and holding them by the corners so they will drip into the waste can. I begin to mop.

"Just get out of here," she says through her teeth. 'You belong in the woods."

-14-

Swollen and bleary

In the early morning I hear a footstep on the porch and before she can knock or ring, I have opened to door to Simone. Her eyes look swollen and bleary. I am so used to seeing her at her best – almost six feet tall with shining dark skin, bright eyes, and grinning mouth. I balk at the sight of her.

"Whatever is wrong?" I blurt out. "Has something bad happened? Oh, no. Not another death in the woods. I don't think I could bear it."

Simone pulls out a tissue and honks into it. "Just a cold. A bad one. Came over me in the night. Ugh." She plops on my couch. "I need tea. Or if you have it, chicken soup. Mothering, please."

I can't tell you how happy I am that Simone has come to me. She looks dreadful and yet I have a big smile on my face.

"Let me check my soup supply. I grabbed a can of chicken noodle the other day and I don't think I've touched it. It's getting to be soup weather," I sing.

Simone makes a croaking noise and asks, "No homemade soup?"

"Well, given a warning I could have homemade soup but Progresso is what you get on short notice. Let me make some tea too. You relax. Sit here at the counter."

I turn to the sink where I struggle with the tabbed can lid, eventually pulling it back but not before spilling about a third of the soup. I shrug and pour it into the pan. Starting the kettle I turn to her, "Tell me what's up. Arrest anyone in the Remy case?"

"No, early days" she bemoans. "Interviewing a lot of people."

"Like who?" I ask.

"Not talking about it."

"Well, I know you talked to a Larry Cloud. How did that go?"

"Do you know Larry? I mean, I know you met John and Margot, but did you see Larry when you were in the office?"

"No, I don't think so," I tell her. "What's he like?"

"Larry?"

"Yep, Larry."

Simone rises. "Let's go to a softer seat." She moves to the sofa.

"He's, well, he's sort of what you would expect of a Larry."

"I don't have expectations of a Larry. You do?"

"I always think the name Larry implies a sort of...well... bland, whitish man."

I smile. "Really? No stereotypes with you! And he was just what you were expecting?"

"Yeah, he's the outside helper there. Clears trails. Mows grass. Probably parks cars during events."

"You know, I bet he was the one on the walkie talkie to John when I first reported the hand. I think John said 'Larry' when he told him to block off the trail and look for the hand."

"Yep, most likely the one."

"Did he give any insightful information?" I probe.

"Nothing I didn't know before. He seemed to be a bit miffed with Margot though. Gave her a dirty look when we both walked out of the office."

"That's easy to understand. Even I find Margot challenging."

Simone raises one eyebrow. "How so?"

"She gives me disapproving looks. She complains about me – I'm too muddy from falling in the creek, I interrupt her endless paper sorting, I spill tea on her carefully collated sheets."

"You spilled tea on her work?" Simone asks, surprised.

"I was being very friendly and the tea cup was hot and, well, these things happen."

"They seem mostly to happen to you."

"Let's change the subject. Did you talk to the cafe woman?"

"A bit. She is tucked away in her area most of the time. I had coffee there. Excellent coffee. I find that's a perk of the job, trying out coffee in various places."

"And what else?" I inquire.

Simone shakes her head. "Nothing now. I'm staying away from the office due to this cold so I am in noodling mode. You know, thinking things over and hoping inspiration will come."

I hear the mail drop in the box outside and go to fetch it. Simone lays down on the sofa. I sigh. Neither Simone nor the mail are providing much stimulation. I head to the kitchen where the kettle has just finished. After pouring tea, I ladle soup. I bring them Simone on a tray.

"Do you want to eat back at the counter or just stay on the sofa?" I ask gently.

"Counter, I think," Simone says. "I don't want to mess up your upholstery."

As Simone stands she takes a sip. "Great tea. Earl Grey?"

"With double bergamot!"

"What's a bergamot?"

"The citrusy flavor they put in the tea to make Earl Grey."

"Hmm. All these years of downing Earl Grey and I knew nothing of bergamot. Some detective I am. Speaking of my job, I do have a question for you."

"Shoot," I reply with enthusiasm.

"Have you run into that fellow who pulled you out of the stream. I need to talk with him. He was close to the body."

"Saw him yesterday."

"What? Where?" Simone croaks out these questions.

"I saw him walking along the stream, under the Ravine Trail. All alone. Balancing at the edge of the water."

"Near the scene of the body? Wait, didn't we speak in the park yesterday? Why didn't you tell me?"

"Yes. I admit I returned there, to the place where the body was. And yes, I did see you but not for very long and it didn't occur to me to tell you."

"Well, first of all there is tape along that trail to keep people away and secondly, maybe I could have caught up with this guy."

"There was tape. Somehow it's down over the edge of the ravine now." I shrug.

"What? I wonder how that happened." Simone blows her

nose. "But you saw the same guy who helped you – camo, beard, big boots, etc.?"

"Yes. It was him."

"So he's still around the park?"

"He was yesterday. You just have to chance upon him. I'm wondering if maybe John, or Margot, or Larry Cloud know him?"

She shrugs, coughs loudly and then settles into her chair. I sit across from her as she tucks into her soup. After only a few spoonfuls, she sighs and puts her hand to her forehead.

"Go on upstairs and lay on the bed in the spare room," I suggest. "Take your tea."

Simone obliges, taking measured steps up the stairs with mug in hand.

I look over the barely eaten soup. "Man, that girl can waste food," I think. "She has a habit of stopping by, asking for tea and food, and leaving before she finishes."

~15~

All confidential

G rabbing the cast off food, I head to the kitchen. As I walk back into the living room I hear Simone open the window in the room upstairs. "Is that a good idea?" I wonder. "The air is brisk." I think about calling to her but just then there is a weak knock on the front door.

I fling open the front door to see Junie on the porch. Junie is a neighbor two doors down. He moved in with Angus Peacock a couple of years ago and they are developing a home software business. Junie is a dear man who has suffered a tragedy and is always welcome.

I peek through the screen door and ask him in but he says "Oh no, my boots are a bit muddy. I just want to ask you a question. Can we stay on the porch?"

I grab a jacket and go out with him. "What's up, Junie?" I ask. "How are things at the end of the street?" I motion for him to sit down.

"As good as they can be," he says. "Angus and I are making good progress with our software and I think this business will be very good for both of us. The thing is, Kate, I sometimes just need to get out of the house. Both of us are in morose states at times. You are always welcoming, here on your front porch, and I hope things are going well for you." He pauses. "Hey, is that Simone's car in the drive? I seem to remember that bumper sticker." He points to the sticker on the back of Simone's car. It's an old fashioned smiley face saying 'Have a nice day.' So un-Simone.

"Yep. She's here. Has a bit of a cold and stopped by for tea and soup. Can I interest you in some tea?"

"Oh no. Just checking in."

"Okay, well let's see. My latest obsession is hiking at Rob Ryan Park. I have stepped off the neighborhood pavement onto dirt trails under trees." I give him a smile. It's good to see him.

"Sounds like more of an adventure than circling the blocks around here. Rob Ryan, huh? I've heard of it. Never been there although I was asked to go walk there by a friend. He was in my grief counseling group and I could tell that he loved that place." Junie drops his head. "I recently heard he died. It seems it's all sadness sometimes. I hope he didn't do himself in from his grief."

"You mean Derek Remy?"

"That's him." Junie looks at me in surprise. "Did you know him?"

"No, but I..." I can barely go on. Should I tell my story to Junie? He is looking at me with such trusting eyes I feel I have to be honest.

"See, I found Derek's body."

"What?" Junie looks as if he's seen a ghost. And maybe he feels he has after our last experience together. He stares at me for a long minute. "You found his body?"

"I was hiking in Rob Ryan."

"Yes, I heard he died there. Which I found very ironic because he loved it there so..."

Again Junie gives me an extended look.

"Ironic, yes," I gulp.

"How odd, you finding his body. Er, I hate to say you have a talent for that but look at the evidence." Junie refers to my macabre history in the neighborhood.

I gulp. "You're right. I may be the harbinger of death. It's embarrassing." I can barely look at Junie now, but I go on. "I slid down an embankment over the creek, it was fast running and I was grasping for a hold and found something to grab onto. And, uh, so sorry to say, but it was Derek's hand. He was buried in the path above and his hand had protruded out the side of the bank. He may have saved me…. after he was dead."

Now Junie stares at me for a full minute. "Up until a few years ago I thought life was fairly predictable. Then the incident in the garden here on Summer Street and all that," he pauses. "And now this. What used to be solid ground has gone all wobbly. And I'm afraid life likes toying with you. My dear girl, I am so sorry. It sounds like an horrific experience."

"Well, yes. Now it seems like a dream, or a nightmare."

"And yet you are hiking over there?"

"I know. I know. But I'm drawn there now. I feel so bad about Derek. Although there is some good news. Simone has been assigned to this case."

"Good luck to her." Junie puts his hand on his chin, thinking. "Derek had a complicated life. He was bashful at first in the group but then it seemed to flood out of him. He came across as a person that analyzed a situation and then made a move. And when he felt comfortable among us all, he opened his heart."

"What did he say, if I may ask. Or is this all confidential?"

Junie considers for a moment. "Derek is gone. Who's confidence would I be protecting? And if someone is trying to solve his death, knowing him better might help. See, he had a lot of people pulling at him and there he was, mourning his wife. He adored her. I understood that."

"What do you mean, people pulling at him?"

"Oh, he had a vision for land that abutted the park. Land that was a family farm that was being sold. He was putting all his focus on buying that land for the park but, unfortunately, he wasn't the only one who had his eye on it. There were developers planning to make a killing by filling the land with mixed use housing, services, eateries – a whole village. And after his wife died I think he doubled his focus on the land. He was forever meeting with the family who owned the farm and laying out plans. They seemed to be dithering about what to do."

"And he revealed all of this in group counseling? Or maybe it's common for people to reveal a lot in counseling. I shouldn't be so quick to judge."

"Some of it, well all of it, he told me when we went for coffee. He and I were the only two who had lost our wives in a sudden, unexpected way. There were a lot of people who went through long illnesses with their loved ones and that took up a lot of counseling time. Well spent, for them, but we didn't really relate to it. So we had coffee, a drink or two. And Derek became verbose after a drink or two."

"This must be such a shock for you, Derek's death."

"When I saw it in the paper I couldn't believe it. It made me feel that everyone I touch dies. I honestly assumed it was suicide when I saw it. But now it seems it was a horrible crime."

"Yes. I believe it was. Still unexplained. Like I said, Simone is working on the case."

"That's good. She'll figure it out. But as I said, he had a lot of people who wanted a piece of him. His brother wanted money. Derek had a lot of it and there was some bad history between them. I never really knew much about it. And apparently Derek's wife was generous with the brother, but Derek didn't feel the same way about helping him out. And it seems she, his wife, was very involved with a new children's private school and had intended to bestow a large endowment – she was a very successful children's author you may know. According to Derek they were trolling for large and ongoing donations. The Derek I knew was a kind, broken person but he seemed such a nice man. He had a lot of people with their hands out, wanting something from him. He wasn't a push over I can tell you that. He could hold his own. He told me a story about…" Junie seems to think better of going on.

Junie and I both stare across the street. Gilda is there, snipping off dead blossoms. Finally Junie comments, "Garden was good this year, huh? Gilda is a busy woman."

"Yep," I say. I think a moment. "See that blueberry bush over there to the right?"

"Not sure. Don't have a feel for blueberry bushes."

"You see the round bush with the little leaves that are turning reddish? I planted that."

"You a blueberry fan?"

"Well, yeah but I did it because Gilda asked me to."

"I've seen you in the garden working with her. Nice of you to help out."

"I find I enjoy it. And she sometimes brings out a glass of wine on a summer evening. I guess that's my payment."

"I'd like to plant something in that garden." Junie stares. I know he is remembering his wife.

"I'll mention it to Gilda. She would like that. Have you seen her daughter? She stops by sometimes. Has a little girl?"

"No, can't say I remember them. I don't have such a view as you."

"Well her daughter, Myra, she is a tough lady. She does a lot of the heavier work for Gilda."

"Must be a big strong girl."

"No, not much bigger than me. But she can dig a hole in the ground! How do you think I got that blueberry bush in there? She dug the hole, I placed the bush in and refilled the soil around it."

"I'll think of it as Kate's blueberries every time I walk by." Junie smiles and rises. "I'm going to move on. I have some thinking to do about what you told me about Derek. I have to come to terms with all of this. And you finding his body, I have to come to terms with that too."

He touches my hand, bows his head gentlemanly, and leaves the porch. I watch him plod up the street.

And then Simone appears inside the front door. "Junie is a wealth of information," she says. "I heard it all through the window."

"I wouldn't have thought Junie's soft voice would have been audible up there."

"If you put your ear to the screen it was. I knew about most of what he said – the major players in Derek's life. But the details and the insight into Derek's personality are helpful. I bet the story he didn't go into had to do with the accusations by his brother-in-law, Rhonda's brother. He never forgave Derek for her death and implied he had a hand in it."

I give Simone a smile. "Despite your cold, you were still alert enough to take advantage of an opportunity to hear about Derek's private conversations."

I pause to think and then point up the stairs. "But you should get back into bed. I have things to do."

"What things?"

I give her a mischievous smile.

"Kate, you make me nervous. Stay out of this. There are desperate people after a murder is committed."

"Don't worry about me. Just take it easy."

I wait for a response but there is none. She slowly climbs the steps and when she disappears at the top, I rub my hands together. I have a great idea to help me organize my thoughts. I whisper to no one, "Time to get busy on my crime board!"

-16-

They all look guilty

I look around the house for a spot for the display of suspects. I am tingling with excitement. After a quick assessment of the downstairs I have it. I'll put the crime board in the dining room. What's a dining room for anyway? I take a piece of particle board about 20 inches by 30 inches and list each suspect. Quietly I tiptoe upstairs to my cramped, rarely used office. I mustn't disturb Simone and I certainly don't want her interfering in my crime board project. One quick peek into the adjoining room to see Simone sleeping and I gently close the bedroom door. I pull up Derek's obituary online. I print out the page and clip out the photo. I know Rhonda's name and I hope to find a photo of her online. Bingo! A lovely headshot. She was beautiful I think. After I get the picture, I read a bit about her and realize the school that she was supporting, the one she planned to leave all her royalties to, has a link on her site. I go there and get a nice logo from the organization. I can't seem to find an image of Derek's brother Dale so I print another of Derek to mock up. And while I'm at it, I reprint Rhonda's photo too. I'll chop of her long hair and make it into her brother. There is some resemblance. I grab a stack of index cards and scotch tape and head down to the dining room.

Half an hour later I have added spots on the board for Rhonda, her brother, Dale Remy, and a general category called 'Developers'. Derek's brother's picture on the board is a copy of Derek's obit photo with a few lines added around the eyes. His eyes made an impression on me at the memorial. Rhonda's brother looks good with his 'haircut'. The developers are shadow people like you see online if you haven't chosen an avatar for yourself. I step back. They all look guilty, I think. I look over my work. Rather amateurish. I shrug. I have limited resources. I need more information on the board and decide to go for a written description of each. I pick up a black marker.

Derek Remy – (Alone at the top of the board.) A philanthropist. A nature lover. The park father. And yet stingy with his brother, stingy with Rhonda's bequest. In a struggle with the developers over the farm… Mourning for his wife. Derek is DEAD.

Dale Remy – Took money from Rhonda and has a past history that divides him and Derek. The brother is DESPERATE. Or SAD? I pause. He seemed nice at the memorial. Maybe he is MISUNDERSTOOD.

Rhonda Remy – Derek's wife. Kind to Dale. Successful children's author. Deceased. Disappeared off the coast of Cape May. Lost at sea. Desperately mourned by Derek. Rhonda is the SAINT.

Rhonda's brother – I wish I had gotten his name. My crime board would be more complete with it. Angry. Spiteful? He is VENGEFUL.

The wannabe farm developers – They were in conflict with Derek over the use of the farm. They see $$$.

This time when I step back I feel proud. I really like my one-word description of each. And then I hear Simone on the stairs. What will she think of this? She enters the dining room, her eyes immediately going to the white particle board with the suspects. I wait for a bit of mocking.

"Good start," is all she says. She walks closer, picking up my marker as she heads over to the board.

"Hang on," I say, worried about protecting my hard work. "I'll do the writing if you don't mind."

She hands me the marker with a slight bow. "Of course. How presumptive of me."

I grab the pen and turn to her, waiting for her input.

Simone thinks and begins. "First of all, Rhonda's brother's name is Michael Sespin. You could find that online if you dig enough. He has been haunting the station with his theories about his sister's death. Really rather dumb as we have no jurisdiction over that death and he only makes himself a suspect in Derek's death. A bit off the rails I would say."

I jot Michael's name on the board.

Simone considers and then points to the board. "I could give you names for the developers, but I am hesitant to do that. They just want to do what they do... develop land and make money. But Derek was determined to preserve the land. Dale told me he hated the idea of those green hills and mature trees being mowed over for more houses. He was working all sides of the funding... the township, the Nature Conservancy, county resources, his own funding, etc. As Junie indicated, Derek was a complicated man. Caring and generous on the one hand, driven when motivated, but then could be stingy with his brother. It depends on who you talk to what picture you get of him."

Simone points to the board. "You need to add the woman from the children's classic school, the Heritage School. The founder's name is Chloe Bedner. The school curriculum is based on art and literature. It focuses on helping underprivileged children to get a classics education."

"Oh, I forgot. I have the school logo here somewhere." I paste it onto the board. I add 'Chloe's Heritage School' under it. Hmm, I think. I bet Chloe is very disappointed that she may not get her endowment. I wonder if she has other benefactors that can muster enough to get the school running? Is Chloe ANGRY? Or just DISAPPOINTED? Or very DETERMINED?

Simone turns to me. "What about the guy who rescued you? I keep thinking about him and the way he behaved. I would say he left the scene of a crime."

"Oh yeah," I exclaim. "Rescue man. He had brown hair and a beard." I grab the marker and draw a stick figure in boots. I stare at my primitive drawing and search for a one word label. SLIPPERY.

Simone laughs. "Yeah, slippery. I get it. He melts away into the forest after he has grabbed your wet hand to pull you from the water while standing on wet rocks."

Her eyes rove over my Crime board. "It's quite a crowd there. The question is, who is responsible for Derek being dead in the woods with a contusion on the side of his head and a rope burn around his neck?"

"Head wound and rope burn? I didn't know."

Simone starts. "Okay, well, keep it under your hat. That might have slipped out but, yeah."

"But he was buried so..."

"Not suicide."

Simone looks over the board. "Our dear, dead Derek is a complicated man. So generous... to a point. So revered... to a point. So loving... to a point." She pauses and looks up at the wall. "You know your crime board is making me think. I'm going to take a little walk around your neighborhood for inspiration. Don't follow me."

Robert's Story 999

It's just after noon. I am thinking about grabbing some lunch when I hear a rap at the door. Simone is standing there with a red nose and tissue in hand.

"Open up!" she demands. "I'm hungry. Are you guys serving food?"

"No, not yet. Not open." I let her in anyway.

"What kind of restaurant is this?" she asks.

"One that is 'Coming Soon.'" I point to the sign on the door.

"I didn't think that applied to me, a friend and public servant."

"OK, well, we have some condiments, a few bags of raw ingredients, and a lot of alcohol. What kind of lunch were you looking for?"

"Not that," she agrees. She looks around and sees Jake and Sebastian across the way. She nods and then turns back to me. "Can I have a designated table? You know, one that's reserved for me."

"You won't be able to afford it," I reply glibly. "This is not a diner or deli. It is a high end bistro."

Just then I hear a key scratching at the door. I look up to see Jim Tucci fussing at the lock. I open the door for him and he charges in, a bit unsteady on his feet.

"I need a drink," he announces. It seems to me maybe he has

already had one. He turns slowly around, arms outstretched. "I can see it. I can feel it. This place is on the verge of greatness! A craft cocktail please!"

Jake takes one look at him and exits to the kitchen, rolling his eyes at me as he goes. I glance over at Sebastian. He is seething. He grabs a rag and begins madly polishing the bar, muttering to me, "Might as well humor him. I have a couple of tweaks I want to make and it's easier to go along with big Jim."

I shrug. I wish 'Big Jim' would stop drinking away the stock. I see movement down behind the bar and lean over to look. By Sebastian's feet sits Simone. She puts her index finger to her lips and then mouths "Distract him." She points up and over to Jim.

I look from Simone to Jim and then to Sebastian who is shaking his head as he shakes a cocktail.

"Jim," I say, "come out and let's go over our plan for signage." We exit the front of the restaurant. When we come back in, I look to Sebastian and he points to the kitchen. Simone has slipped out the back.

~17~

How suspicious could he be

As I close the dryer door I hear someone ring the doorbell. What fresh hell is this, I think.

And there is Simone, waiting impatiently at the door, back again.

"You can just come in with a 'yoohoo' you know. You don't have to ring that bloody bell."

Simone barges through the door. I stand back and ask her "How was your stroll?"

"An important matter. Jim Tucci is at this moment in Robert's restaurant and.."

"Officially it will be called Bistro on High," I interrupt.

"Yeah, well, whatever. He is trying out cocktails – is that a thing – and they are having their effect. He's looks like a guy who could get sloppy. But he knows me, I've talked to him. He'll clam up if I'm there."

"What do you mean, 'get sloppy'? About the case? If you so need to listen to him, isn't there another detective you could send? A colleague? Someone who Jim hasn't met?"

"No, time is short and getting someone here would be difficult. I'll talk to Robert later, maybe he will have heard something intriguing". She raises her eyebrows. "Anyway, I gotta go to another thing." She shrugs. "I'll figure something out." As she walks toward the door she gives me a happy wave. The door shuts and I am rocked by the sound of an explosive sneeze.

As I fold the laundry, I feel disquieted, pensive. I get that Simone would like to catch anyone revealing details he shouldn't have. But what information would Jim have? I pause and take another look at the crime board. When did Simone talk to Jim? What would Jim know? I sit on the sofa and stroke my chin in thought. Maybe he is one of the developers? He invested in the restaurant so he puts money in business ventures. Oh, interesting. Then I say to myself out loud, "I don't have anywhere to be. I could walk down. How suspicious could he be of me?" I smile. "No time to waste."

-18-

Get off my lawn

A s I head down the porch steps, I practice a little. "'Hey, Jim, anything you want to say about Derek Remy?' No. I need to be cooler than that. Maybe I'll bring up the park, say I just came from there, and fit into the conversation that I found a body in the mud. Maybe even that I found the body." I stop mid-sidewalk. "You can do this!"

Continuing my rehearsal, I walk slowly down one block and then another "Hi Jim. Good to see you. Had a great walk today over at Rob Ryan Park. You've heard of it, right? Sad how they found that body. Did you know Derek? Did you hate Derek?" I stop just outside the restaurant, realizing I'm not ready for this. I consider going next door for a cappuccino as a delay tactic. It's tempting as two coffees just walked by me, smelling so good. I look ruefully up the street as the aroma fades away. I look at the restaurant again then take a step back. I want to go back home but I am convinced that Simone needs me. I look in the bistro window and see Jim gesturing as he talks. Big gestures and then a big laugh. I gulp.

When I enter the restaurant, Robert is standing behind the bar with Sebastian. Jim is leaning on the counter having finished whatever exciting story he was telling. They are eying each other uncomfortably in the silence. After a deep breath, I call out gaily, "Hi all. Was walking by and thought I'd say hi!"

Jim turns to me and I can see he recognizes me. He likes to stop by and see how his investment is coming along. He seems to think he can take over when he's here. At least that's how Robert, Bobby, and Sebastian feel, but they are in no position to complain to him.

"You're Robert's mother, aren't you?" he begins. "Come here often?"

This puts me off. Is it a problem that I sometimes stop by? I hesitate and Jim holds a glass up high and says, "Try out this 'Get Off my Lawn' drink." He burps quietly. Simone can read a drunk.

"Well thanks, sounds good." He hands me the glass and I take a sip.

"Yummy," I say as I turn to Jim. "I pass by here when I take my daily walk in the neighborhood – I live just a few blocks away. So sometimes I stop in, but not a lot. It's just that it's on my walking route and so…"

"You're a walker, huh? Me, I'm a sitter." He gives a big laugh and takes another gulp. I don't think I like him much.

He goes on. "This place is shaping up. These guys are doing a great job." He sweeps his arm to indicate Sebastian and Robert. "Actually, if I lived here I might take up walking just to stop by and see what these fellows are concocting." He gives a big laugh.

I take the plunge. "Sometimes I go to Rob Ryan Park for my walk. It's lovely there."

"Oh, yes," Jim barks. "Rob Ryan Park. I've been there. A lot of trees and mud and bugs if you ask me."

"Oh, I guess," I stammer. "I like it there."

"Whatever," Jim retorts, then turning back to Sebastian, "You are a magician sir. This drink is fabulous."

He hiccups. I can't believe it. He actually hiccups. Somehow this bolsters my courage. Why am I timid around this fool?

"As I was saying, I find Rob Ryan Park soothing. Sublime really." I give Jim a big smile. He smiles back. I consider how to get to the subject of Derek Remy. After a bit, I plow forward.

"Of course, Jim, I have to admit the park has had its problems. An, um, incident."

"I know all about that. It was a big incident. A man was buried in the mud in that park. And I knew him. He also loved that park and see where it got him."

I turn to Sebastian. "This is a good drink. Anymore we can taste?" I look at Jim and give him a wink.

"I want to try a pink one next," Jim cries with sudden enthusiasm.

I continue with my gambit.

"Yes, um, that's it. The incident I mean. So sad and so unusual. And you knew him? You must be devastated. I heard his name was Derek something?"

"Derek Remy! I sure did know him. Pain in the ass. Sticking his nose in where he shouldn't. And now it seems someone knocked him off. Big surprise."

"Murder?!" I say, awestruck. "Really. Who would do such a thing?" I venture.

"Don't know. Don't want to speculate. I won't miss him or his tree hugger friends. I wonder who gets his money now?"

"His money? What do you mean?"

"He was a rich sonofabitch who had nothing better to do than cause trouble. He was a problem for my development company."

"So you two didn't see eye to eye? Were you enemies?"

"No. I don't know. But he may have pushed someone a little too hard and they bumped him on the head or something. Not exactly sure what happened but he was buried in the park in the mud. How about that! Just goes to show you."

"What?"

"Huh?" Jim eyes are a bit bleary now and I think his focus is off.

"What goes to show you?"

"Don't mess with people. They can get together and do you in!" He looks back at Sebastian. Robert had gone into the back room. He blinks heavily.

"Forget the pink drink. I'm outta here."

He stumbles toward the door where Sebastian grabs him and sits him down. "I'm calling you a ride. Give me your keys."

Jim drops his keys in Sebastian's hand and plops into a chair. I sit down next to him. I decide to put the screws to him.

"I found the body," I confess. "I was the one who discovered it."

He blinks hard. "Oh yeah?"

"Yeah. I know a bit more about his death than you might think."

"What? What do you know?"

"How he died."

Jim's eyes get big and he looks at me, at least the best he can with his unfocussed stare.

I continue. "The police are hot on the trail of someone or some people. That I know."

"How do you know?" Jim suddenly seems more alert.

"You find a body, you talk with the police, you are there when they dig it up, you know. Information gets leaked."

"What information?"

I look out the window. "Your ride is here. See you soon." As I walk out into the street I think how much fun it will be to tell Simone about my sleuthing and about Jim's statement 'Don't mess with people. They can get together and do you in!'

Robert's Story IV

Bobby and I are reworking the menu items when Sebastian comes into the kitchen. Bobby looks over at him and says, "Is that jackass gone?"

Sebastian grins and deadpans, "Don't call Robert's mother a jackass!"

Looking confused, Bobby turns to me and then back at Sebastian. "I have no idea what you're talking about, barman. I know I heard Jim out there. Were you plying him with alcohol?"

"Not really. I was mixing up some drinks, finalizing the opening day options, and he came in, jumped on a bar stool and asked to try one out." Sebastian couches the truth a bit to Bobby. "One thing lead to another, and let's just say, he gave some good feedback on a drink before chugging down the remaining liquor in a couple of glasses. Made him a bit loopy."

Sebastian continues. "And then," he points at me, "your mother came in and started up a conversation with him that veered to the park where that body was found. Apparently they both knew the guy. In fact, I sort of feel like your mother was egging Jim on to find out what he knew about the dead man. And, I almost forgot, your mother said she found the body! That can't be true."

"Oh, but it is," I say forlornly. "You have no idea the adventures my retired mother can have on any ordinary day. On the day she discovered the body in the park, she was falling down a steep embankment into a creek and when she grasped for something to stop her fall, she ended up holding the hand of a dead person who was buried in the ground above. So to be clear, she didn't find a body, she found a hand. Later they discovered a body was attached."

Bobby and Sebastian stare open-mouthed.

"Really?" Only Bobby can manage to speak.

"Really," I retort.

"Are they still out there?" Bobby manages to ask, pointing out toward the bar.

"No," Sebastian cuts in, "I herded Jim out of here in an Uber and took his keys. Then your mother left as the Uber pulled out. Jim will be back for those keys sometime. They're under the bar near the sink."

All three of us are quiet for a few moments.

"What did Jim say about the park and the body?" I finally speak.

"That he knew the guy and he was a jerk and he knows some people that will be glad he's dead."

Robert and Bobby look at Sebastian. "Wow. Nasty." Bobby shakes his head.

"I thought the deceased was a nice guy," I chime in. "Big philanthropist. Park supporter. That's what I heard about him anyway."

Sebastian frowns. "Well, he's a goner now – whether he was a saint or sinner." He pauses a minute, thinking. "It was a weird scene, man. Your mom comes in, starts talking with Jim, and they immediately start discussing this body in the park. I'm not even sure how it came up in the first place."

I shrug, but I know exactly how it came up. It stank of Simone and Mom.

-19-

The mint tea was delicious

The next morning I am back in the park at the cafe to try the coffee. It is as delicious as Simone said. Junie is going to join me outside in the parking lot in a half hour. He came by and said he wanted to see the park where Derek died. The one Derek had talked so much about. So we set up to meet today.

I have time to enjoy coffee before I meet him. I'm at the small bar area where you can lean on your elbows and watch the manager/barista at work. I notice she has a small, rectangular metal pin that, when the lights don't glare over the words, reads 'Tory, Cafe Manager'. The menu is interesting – does Tory cook too? Looking up, I can see there is a doorway to another room. Must be a kitchen. The food is simple. Sandwiches, soup, breakfast items, salads, pastry. Must be a short order type cook. But someone must be simmering the soups. I catch Tory's eye when she is in a lull and wave her over. I wonder if she remembers me.

"The mint tea was delicious but I love this coffee," I gush. "So fresh and smooth. I'll bet every time I'm in the park I won't be able to resist stopping in here for a cup. Are you the cook too?"

Tory gives me a distracted smile. "I do most of the work here. It's my place. Well, I think of it that way. The park owns it but I've been hired to run it. I have a lot of free rein about what I serve."

"Well, you're doing a bang up job if you ask me."

"Thanks."

"How do you manage it all by yourself? You must live here."

"I have some part time help. And Kevin runs the grill. He's here with me most of the time. We're only open from eight until three. And we're closed Monday." She pauses. "You look familiar."

I ignore her. "I bet John and Margot stop in for a beverage now and then."

"Oh, you know John?"

"Not really. Had an encounter with him over a, um, trail incident."

"Was it Larry?"

"Larry, no. But I've heard about Larry."

"What did you hear?"

"Just that a man named Larry Cloud works here. Nothing more."

"Good. I mean, he does a lot of the outside maintenance and I just think that, well, that he should be a bit more invisible to park visitors. That's why I was surprised when you said you heard about him." She wipes at the counter. With a turn of her head she eyes me. "Who are you? I know we've met before but... Did you know Derek? He died here in the park."

"I know, I'm the one who found the body – or, noticed there was a body."

"Really? And you're just sitting here talking about it like it was a normal occurrence?"

"Oh, I never thought it was a normal occurrence."

"I bet." She gives me a glare. I seem to be unable to get along with any employees in this park.

She goes on. "You know Margot? She works in the office out there. I overheard her talking about that awful day. You're the muddy woman. Gee, why are you here? That experience would drive me away for good."

"You would think," I begin, but Tory shakes her head slowly. "I don't understand people."

I watch her walk away. John enters the cafe as she ducks behind the counter. He raises his hand in a big hello and Tory beckons him. The two of them have a whispered exchange where John glances at me. I grab my coffee and head out. It seems I am public enemy number one in this building.

-20-

Not my job

"Yoo hoo!"

As I exit the building after my encounter with Tory, Cafe Manager and John, Park Administrator, I see my friend.

"Simone!" I exclaim. "Good to see you. Hard at work on the body-in-the-trail case?"

"Sadly, yes."

"Getting anywhere?"

"We're combing the park, talking to people."

"People in there?" I point toward the building. "I was just thinking how I seem to have offended everyone that works in this building. I try to be nice. It bugs me that they don't like me."

"Your encounters with the staff here are not my job. And you really need to stop worrying whether people like you. Big hint. You keep finding dead bodies, people won't like you. Anyway, I'm trying to figure out how that poor man ended up like he did. The staff knew him, to be sure, but he promoted and financially supported the park which was only to their benefit. So leave me out of your personal vendettas."

"Apparently Margot, chief paper sorter, has discussed my

demeanor after I found the body with Tory from the cafe. And not favorably."

Simone lets out a laugh. "She does sort a lot of papers, doesn't she? I think her real job is to keep an ear out about what is going on in the park. Her hands are moving papers about, but her eyes and ears are taking it all in. I think you're confusing office gossip with maliciousness. These people work together all the time so what happens here is fodder to them."

Simone gives me a wave and walks off. I'm sure she's right. My feelings have been hurt because these people don't like me. I want everyone to like me.

-21-

A rope dangling

I leave the personalities at the park office behind and meet Junie outside. We walk to the beginning of the Old Farm Trail and companionably, stroll to the Trillium Trail, traversing most of the park. We finally come to the bottom of Bunny Hill and, side by side, climb up to the top. It's mostly open with long grass but tall trees sway here and there. At the top, there are five or six very large trees, one of which has a rope dangling from it. Junie and I both look at the rope and then at each other. Maybe kids swing here, I think, but I would assume the park doesn't want such dangerous activity. Do they monitor these trails? I sit down in the grass, looking northward, my hands grasping my knees. A gentle wind plays with my hair. Junie stands and checks out the dangling rope.

As I gaze over the park, I see two people milling about in Bird Meadow below. One is bending over to examine something. Her stance reminds me of Simone's when she is intrigued by a clue or possible evidence. When Simone is on a case, she has a determined look about her. Maybe it's the set of her jaw. She looks like someone you don't want to cross. I smile as I think about how I have come to think of Simone almost like a daughter in these past couple of years.

When we first met after the crime in my neighborhood, she was missing her mother intensely. It was only a few months before that she had lost her. I now understand that, underneath her tough veneer, Simone is a lost woman. And as the case went on, I began to feel such caring for her. Since then she has stopped by often. On occasion she used to join Robert and me for our weekly dinners out back when he was living here. She played Trivial Pursuit with us on Christmas Eve. I have found her asleep on my porch swing after I came home from a day away. Simone has enriched my life and I hope I do the same for her. I never thought I would be another witness to another crime. But here I am, again, involved in one of her cases.

The two people have moved out of sight. A man enters the meadow on a utility vehicle. Must be a park worker, I think.

"You know, Junie," I call to him. "Maybe that's the Larry guy I never met." He's too far away to see well. And I'm too content here on my hill to hike down to meet him. I add, "Maybe he will be the worker who likes me."

Junie gives me a confused look.

I explain. "I didn't make a good impression on the staff when I arrived muddy into their offices. It was after the incident when I discovered Derek."

Junie nods and looks down. We sit quietly for a few minutes.

"We can sort of spy on people from up here."

Junie smiles at me.

As we sit staring out to the horizon, three men walk into view. They are quite far away, past the ball fields that lie ahead.

They look to be somewhere between the adjacent farmland and the park. The land that Derek was trying to get instead of the developers. They are all dressed in dark suits. At least that's what it looks like from here. It's odd to see people in suits out in the park. What are they up to? I turn to Junie.

"See those three men over there?" I point.

He squints. "Yes. They look out of place even though they're the size of ants from up here."

"I think they might be the three men who want to develop the land over there. Did you know there was contention between land developers and Derek? Maybe they're up to no good." I look at Junie and raise my eyebrows. "Maybe they're snooping around the park. I think they're inside the park boundaries now." I squint. "Yep, they are definitely moving into the park area."

Junie looks harder. "Can't really tell anything from here. But I remember Derek did talk about expanding the park. He said something about being in competition with a group who wanted the land he was planning to use. He called them evil. I didn't understand. Sounded hyperbolic to me."

I think about the word 'evil'. Derek used that to describe his competitors?

"I'm taking a picture," I announce and pull out my phone and aim it at the men far away in the distance. "It's suspicious, no?" I quiz Junie. "Three men in dark suits walking into a park. Maybe they're snooping around or maybe they're coming back to the scene of their crime."

Junie nods. "Now that you say that, they do look really suspicious, three dark clad figures moving into the park."

We look at each other and smile. "Our imaginations may be running away with us," Junie observes.

"I'm taking a photo anyway." I move my fingers on the screen to enlarge the image. "I can't get the image large enough to see them well but I bet a police department has a way of really closing in on images. This pic is going to Simone." I make a couple of touches on my phone and the image flies through space to her.

I turn to Junie. "This is why I come to the park a lot now. To see if anything untoward is happening. And now I've seen this."

Junie gives me a wry look.

I glance again at the figures in the distance and say, "I'm ready to get moving. C'mon."

Junie waves me away like a circling gnat. "I'm staying a while. I find I like it here very much."

"But can you find your way out? Back to your car?"

He nods slowly. "All your talk has me up for an adventure but, yes, I can retrace our steps."

I pat his arm and leave.

-22-

Call declined

Alone, I descend Bunny Hill thinking about the three men. I can't wait to hear more from Simone. I get back on the Trillium Trail. I wander onto the Milkweed Trail that goes through the butterfly gardens. There are some Goldenrod and Black-eyed Susans. The carpet of pink, blue, and yellow of spring is gone. I lament that I never made it out here this spring. The breeze is bobbing the Susans' heads. I pat one on its crown. "Pretty girl," I say aloud. Then I hear a guffaw from the woods. "Junie?" I call. I scan the edge of the gardens into the trees where I hear rustling. "Who's there?" I take off toward the sound. No one. I listen and wait. When I hear the noise in the brush ahead to the left, I bushwhack over that way. It's not easy going but I am determined to find the person who laughed. I stop and swivel my head. There's a hand holding a branch a little way ahead! I try to run toward it but the underbrush holds me back, and then I see a tree next to me with accessible branches for climbing. I look up into the yellow leaves and realize that, if I fall and can't grab my phone, I could lay out here for a long time. Dejected, I head to the garden. "I don't like being spied on," I say loudly. "I hope you hear me." I walk on for a while before realizing that I have missed the opening to the garden area. How did I not notice it? All I can see is trees and more trees. I turn in a circle and realize I am lost.

Stumbling about, I come upon a small clearing. I ponder at how I can be lost in a park surrounded by access roads and including a large structure. I just have to listen for other people to stroll by or a car to ramble down one of the roads. Becoming very still, I quiet my breath and listen. I hear a light ping, followed by another and another. It's raining. As I ponder my next move, I feel a sudden chill in the air. When I open my palm to the sky, I feel the raindrops. It is raining harder and people don't generally hike in the rain. If I'm wet, I'll get cold. I sit down on the grass in frustration but of course it only serves to make me wetter. I try to retrace my route in my head remembering any turns I made and the location of the climbing tree I passed. I bolster my reserves, and, convinced I won't die in the woods, I stand calmly. It is at this point that I realize I need a bathroom. This is getting better and better, I think. Lost, cold, wet, need to pee. As I'm trying to make a plan, I hear a child's delighted voice screaming, "I'm dancing in the rain!" I look upward to give a thank you to the heavens and then turn toward the voice. I wave my hands and call, "I'm a bit off the trail and could use some help getting back on course. Can you see me?"

There is rustling and a child grabs my hand and commands, "Over here." He pulls me to the trail where his parents are standing. They appeared confused that their son pulled a full grown woman from the woods. The boy, about ten years old with lovely, bright red hair, seems more in charge than his parents. He's looking at me curiously while they are gaping.

"He rescued me," I announce. "I was lost off trail and he found me. Quite a hero!" The man and woman continue staring at me as if I am an apparition. Their son chirps, "That was fun!"

I chuckle at how pleased he is with himself. "We should all get out of this rain." I glance at the parents. "Could you maybe just point me in the direction of the Administration Building?"

Of course the youngster is the one who answers, and with authority. "It's this way along the trail about ten minutes away. We only just came from there. We're heading back to our car parked on the other end of this trail."

Just then a phone rings. We all look at each other in astonishment. It's obvious it's not in anyone's pocket or backpack but in the brush. The proficient boy leaps towards the sound and to everyone's amazement, returns with a ringing phone. It is a current model in a black case. There is a number appearing on the phone but, to my frustration, the boy taps 'Call declined.'

"But," I begin. "Why didn't you answer it?"

"It wasn't for me," the boy announces. The parents smile at me smugly.

"But it was lost, and by answering it we could have found who it belonged to!"

"Oh," says my little friend, "I didn't think of that." He turns the phone over in his hand, admiring it and pleased he has 'his own' phone.

"Ok, well, I'm headed to the Administration building so I'll drop it off in case someone is looking for it. And someone must be."

I reach my hand out for the phone but the boy pulls it into his chest.

"Finders Keepers!" he exclaims. He bows his red head in protection of the phone. I'm thinking to let him keep it, just as his father walks up and puts out his hand. "Jerry, this is too expensive of an object to claim."

The boy keeps his head down but hands the phone to his dad. I think he's about to cry.

I extend my hand and the father turns it over to me.

"If I didn't say it before, thank you," I call as I step away from them. "Enjoy your hike!" As I look back, the boy is following his parents along the path but looking back at the phone with longing.

I consider and head back toward the little family. "Hey, what's your name? I can give them your name in the office and if no one claims it, I really think it will be Finders Keepers."

He scampers back to me and says proudly, "Jerry Lucas".

"Do you have a phone number?" I am querying the parents now.

The mother looks at the father who sighs and blurts, "555-212-2323."

I repeat this number and cross my fingers at the child indicating I wish him luck.

He turns and ushers his parents down the trail pointing out the correct path on the turn ahead. I think they created a little woodsman and they don't quite know how to handle him. The thought keeps me amused until I reach the building.

As I stride into the entryway, I push my wet hair out of my eyes. There are a few people here drying out from the rain. Margot isn't at her post so I step behind the counter and rap on John's door. He calls loudly, "Come in."

Opening his office door, I peer in. He pulls a face at me.

"What now?" he asks looking at his watch. "I don't have time for this."

"For a lost phone in the woods?" I reply. "It was found ringing in the brush along the Milkweed Trail. A lovely little outdoorsy boy found it. Unfortunately he was unable to take the call, so I am bringing it to you in case someone reports it missing." I pass the phone to him. With a startled expression, he grabs the phone from my outstretched hand.

"I'll take that," he says somewhat gruffly. "Go on now."

"But the boy wants me to give his name and number in case no one claims it. He was enthralled with the phone and feels he should get it back if unclaimed."

John Logan shakes his head. I wait. He looks up and considers.

"OK, sure, give me the information. If no one asks about it, it's his. Tell him not to get his hopes up."

"I doubt I will ever see little Jerry Lucas again, but if I should encounter him on a trail, I will pass along your message." I give John a nod and exit.

What is it about that man that exhausts me?

~23~

He's a vicar

The bathroom is busy and I have to use the far stall. I suppose the woods have emptied due to the rain and this is the logical place to take shelter. As I busy myself, I can hear a low, muffled conversation from the other side of the wall. I think about the layout in the lobby. The men's room is on the far side of the entryway. As I get ready to check out of the stall, I realize that the offices would be on the back side of this wall. So John and Margot and Larry Cloud could be having a conversation which can be heard through the wall. I stop to ask myself why this kind of tickles me and have to admonish myself for childishness. But they did get under my skin a bit and knowing that their conversations are bleeding into the bathroom rather amuses me.

I glance over to the office suite as I exit. No Margot at the counter. No one in sight. I'd better get myself out of here before I cause another embarrassing incident. I can't help a smile as I push open the door to exit.

Things have improved in the weather department. Since the sun has broken through the clouds, the woods are beckoning. I step off onto the Trillium Trail which will connect with the Milkweed Trail. I like the yellow tint to the forest at this time of year and I need cheering up. As I look about me, I begin humming. The trail is narrow here but will soon open up as I near the wildflowers. A chipmunk dashes across the path, the stripes on his back a blur as he rushes on his mission. My mission is to see fall flowers, I think. I pick up the pace and the cadence of my humming. Soon the forest opens, bit by bit, and I begin to see the edge of the small meadow enclosed in the woods.

When I come full into the open field I notice a woman sitting on the edge. She is peering at what looks like a trail map, squinting at it and turning it about. I approach. After my experience in these woods, I feel a responsibility to pay the young boy's kindness forward.

"Hello," I say, somewhat gaily I think. "Looking over the map?"

She looks up. I see a fairly young woman with blond hair and a ruddy, somewhat uneven complexion.

"Oh," she says, "I am trying desperately to position myself on the map. It seems a bit of a jumble."

Her accent is British which surprises me. "The map is rather small and hard to read." I take it from her hands asking "Do you mind?" It's crumpled and the small labels are impossible.

"It sounds as if you are from England," I comment. "Moved here or visiting?"

"Oh, visiting. My first trip here."

"And Pittsburgh was your desired destination?" I ask.

"My husband is at a conference nearby. A religious one. He's a vicar."

"Very nice. And you came along for the fun or you have a mission here too."

"Not missionaries… no, no. Just a chance for John, my husband, to touch base with other denominations and ways of, er, 'vicaring'. And so I came along to see the sights. I didn't realize we would be so far from the city. It is quite suburban here."

"Yep. It sure is. Sorry you're disappointed."

"Oh, no, not really. It's just that I have to entertain myself for a number of days and, since I like rambling, I thought this park was a good place to start. And the hotel is close by."

"I think you made a good choice," I say confidently. "I enjoy this park. Since I am retired I have time to ramble."

"My main occupation is being a vicar's wife, which is busy." She gives a reluctant smile.

I smile back. "Well, I might as well introduce myself. I am Kate…Kate Ranier. Local girl." I chuckle at this description of myself.

"And I am Sarah Jane Pratt. Of Somerset. And I'm lost in the woods and terrified of having to get into the rental car and find my way back to the hotel. It's only a mile or so but driving here is all backward for me."

"Oh, Sarah Jane," I smile, truly enjoying this exchange. "I'm glad to help you. You are heading to…?"

"My car," she sighs. "I need to get back. I almost killed myself on the way over here because I was on the wrong side of the road after I turned and everyone was honking. I 'm not sure how I ever made it."

I grin. I remember driving in England. "OK, well let's get

you back to your car and safely in your hotel. Where is the car, do you know?"

"Near that large brick building with the offices inside. I grabbed a map there and was almost bowled over by a large woman tearing out of the office. That set my nerves off so I found myself darting into the woods. Foolhardy."

"That would probably be Margot." I can see her in my mind's eye.

"Oh, Margot," Sarah Jane says with interest. "I heard, well I was in a bathroom stall but sound carried. I heard someone say 'Margot, you better mind what you do and say.' It was rather mean. And then she replied that she wasn't the problem and then I went over to the sink and washed my hands so I couldn't hear more and then was almost knocked over by, well, Margot."

I turn to Sarah Jane. "I apologize as a local for the despicable behavior. I'll get you to the car. Follow me along the trail."

And so Sarah Jane and I trip along the Trillium Trail until we arrive at our destination. She points out her car.

"And you're parked right next to me!" I exclaim. "I don't usually park in this lot but lucky I did. Do you know how to get to the hotel from here?"

"Yes. No. Perhaps. I hope to recognize landmarks."

"What's the name of the hotel."

"The Radnor."

I pull out my phone and open the maps. "Oh, it's very close. I can give you easy directions."

When I look back at Sarah Jane, I see that her lip is quivering.

"I'm terrified." A tear runs down her face.

I think a moment and then pronounce, "I'll lead you there. Just follow my car."

Sarah Jane, looking as if she has seen the Messiah, grabs my hand and pulls me to her, hugging me. I back away and smile at her. "It's the least I can do for a friend," I say.

Sarah Jane and I both get in our cars and I pull ahead of her. She closely follows me. I signal each turn ahead of time and wait for traffic to clear so we can pull out together. I lead her into the left lane and sit in the turn lane with my signal on. She does the same. When the coast is clear, we pull into the hotel lot in tandem.

After parking, Sarah Jane rushes from her car and knocks on my car window. "Oh thank you so much. Thank you, thank you." She looks at her watch. "I have it is five o'clock here, is that right?"

"Yep," I agree. "I hope you made it back in time for your evening activities."

"Oh my, plenty of time. Nothing starts until 7:30. Would you let me buy you a drink? There is a lovely bar here and I want to show my appreciation." She gives me a hopeful look.

"I would be honored," I reply with an exaggerated bow. "I'd like to get to know you a little better Sarah Jane Pratt. A woman who seeks out hiking trails is a friend of mine."

Robert's Story V

O h, man. I have been setting up interviews, sitting in on interviews, and putting together procedures the last couple of days. There are always personality rifts kicking up here and there and I need to get out for a bit. When patrons are eating here, at least my focus won't be on Bobby and Terrance et al. I hope. I head out the door to my place sucking in the cool air. Everything was washed clean by the brief shower earlier today. I look around at the pavement and brick buildings and cars impatiently idling at traffic lights and I realize – I need to get out in the woods. There is time before dark, and even if I have to stumble out of the park in low light, it will be worth it.

I've already decided it will be Rob Ryan Park. It has to be. After Mom's stories, I need to hike and investigate, look over the Ravine Trail. I run up the stairs to my apartment, grab my hiking boots and a map of the park, and hit the road.

I park in the upper fields area. I'll take the long way over to the Ravine Trail and the administrative building. Old Farm Road past the Monarch Trail. Fresh air; colorful sunset accumulating. A couple and their dog approach so I slow down in order to greet the pup. He nuzzles my hand and kicks his back leg up as I rub his ears. They move on and there is the Trillium Trail on the left. I turn and take it, doubling back a bit to get to the Milkweed Trail then the Ravine Trail. I know this park well. It feels like an old friend right now. My boots crunch leaves. I am briefly blinded as the sun pokes around a tree trunk. Soon the flower field appears on my left and then the beech trees show up on the other side and then fields and courts ahead along with the large brick building. But I turn on the Ravine Trail before I get there. I want to follow it along the creek. I want to imagine a woman sliding down the embankment and landing in the water. And, maybe, I will see evidence of a body being removed from the trail.

Looking for signs of police presence, I walk slowly along the path. It's still muddy, but not bad. I peer over the edge here and there. Man, it looks like a big drop. Gives me a chill. I picture a slight woman sliding down the hill. Hitting the water. How did she walk away from that? As I stare downward, something catches my eye to the front and left. It is a bit of yellow police tape. I lean over the edge gingerly, not wanting to re-enact the 'big fall'. After I grab it, I look at the trail more carefully. It looks like the ground was disturbed here. This is the place.

As I pull in the eight inch piece of yellow plastic tape between my hands, the sun shifts, darkening the woods. I want to be off the trail. It's making me tense and I need to leave it behind. I want to be inside so I head to the administration building.

The door opens with ease. Looking ahead, I see a lobby with a gray linoleum floor. It's a wide space. Bathrooms flanking on the right and left. Information racks on the right. A doorway, somewhat hidden further up to the right which says 'Cafe' above it. Straight ahead, intensely reading something on a white page, stands a middle aged woman. She notices me and drops the paper. Oh, I bet this is the woman my mother says hates her.

As I look toward her she calls, "Helloo! Can I help you?" She gives me a big smile and a small wave.

"Oh, no. Just perusing." I give her a slight smile. "Not too busy in here."

"No, getting late. But I am always happy to help a man in hiking boots." She walks forward.

I involuntarily step backward.

"I'm Margot," she coos. "And you are..."

"Robert."

"Welcome. Do you visit our little park often?"

I start. I squint. She's flirting with me. She doesn't seem to hate me.

"Yep. Don't often come in here though." I find myself taking a step backward. "Gotta go. Light failing."

I point through the doors.

"Well, the parking lot is lit," she says with some satisfaction.

"But I'm parked at the upper fields – across the park. Need to tramp down a few trails to get back." I smile and start to open the door.

"Oh, I've never been over there," she replies. "Is it far? Do you need a ride?"

Her smile keeps getting bigger.

"No, I can make it."

I look at the map in my hand and walk back toward her.

"Here, take a look. In fact, take a walk over sometime. It's a great park."

And then I dodge for the door.

~24~

People murder for money

Sarah Jane and I settle in at a hightop table at the bar and each order a glass of wine. We talk about favorite hikes – many of mine in the western US or in New England. Hers are all about moors. She loves to hike over moors or anywhere she has a vista of moors. I must admit, I find moors quite majestic. She describes her favorite parks in England. Two in particular – one in northeast England called North York Moors National Park and one in Devon in the southwest called Dartmoor. She tells me about her rambling – her term for hiking – and about the club she belongs to. They meet in different national parks or go to local parks. They do the first part of the walk, break for a snack, and then ramble on to the end.

"What I love about the moors," she laments, missing them, "is how the clouds steal the sun for a while and then a shadow rolls across the landscape, changing the colors as it goes only to have the sun reappear and trigger reversal of light and color. And, what I like the best about my ramblers group is the variety of ages and backgrounds of the ramblers. It's a very eclectic crowd and you learn so much about people." She gives one her sweet smiles.

"I think I would like that very much," I say. "Rambling sounds fun and you paint a glorious picture of the moors."

Then Sarah Jane describes the characters in her village. "Our postman, a very nice fellow, but he can't stop himself whispering about any suspicious item of mail he has delivered in the village." She clucks her disapproval, but with a smile on her face. "And there is always a couple sneaking around thinking no one knows what they're up to, but of course we all know of their antics. And," she pauses for dramatic effect, "every year at the village fete, the lady who manages the tea tent sits behind her counter with a porcelain tea cup which contains something stronger than tea. The entire village wagers over when she will drop off to sleep. The local pub owner runs the betting. Really, the poor woman has a problem and everyone is trying to profit from it. But I must say," Sarah Jane gives me a sheepish look, "I have put a few quid into the pot myself." This causes me to choke in laughter. After a few minutes I compose myself and reveal that my vision of a small English village usually revolves around a murder.

"You read too many English mysteries, although I must admit I think ours are the best. But, and this is hard to break to you, there has never, to my knowledge, been a murder where I live. I've seen some scuffles outside the pub and once my neighbor's elderly father went missing in the local woods, but all ended without major mishap.

As the conversation goes on and the level of our wine gets lower, we find we are fast friends. I am sorry to leave but she has a schedule to keep. As I pull out of the parking lot, I am moved to pop into the park on the way home. After all, I go right by it.

I'm relaxed after my glass of wine and I think that mood coupled with being under the trees in the dimming light will cap the day off nicely. I won't think about Derek or his possible murderers. I will think of the park as I used to – a great getaway into nature. I park at the upper fields. It seems baseball practice is just ending. I guess they play spring and fall. Is that Robert's car parked by the backstop? Can't be, I think. After exiting the car, I walk up an embankment at the side of one of the fields. The view opens up and I look over at part of the farm that Derek wanted to annex to the park. It occurs to me that I was drawn here by the siting of the three men dressed in dark suits. I glance around but don't see anyone meeting that description. What I do see are rolling hills and waving grasses. Man, this is lovely land. I never really looked at the view from this spot before. There could be lovely trails through those fields. And I see a pond. Maybe it's stream-fed. I am enraptured by the dancing grasses and the angled shadows of the clouds moving over the fields.

As the wind blows my hair, I feel a kinship with Derek in wanting to preserve this land. I sigh. The sky darkens as the sun disappears for a few minutes. The shadows go away. And with that, my mood darkens as well. Now I envision rows of houses, their roofs following the contours of the hills. I see them as a sea of light gray siding with darker gray roofs, roads winding among them. And maybe it goes to an area of concentrated lights. Lights for the services. At night, you might even see the lights of the houses and the shops from the park. I understand why Derek tried to save this land. Did it result in his death?

I plop down in the grass to think. So we have two sides – Derek the nature lover who wanted to expand the park and …

oh wait.. keep his house nestled in woods and open fields. And the other side who saw dollar signs in developing the land. Lots of zeros after the dollar signs. I think Simone is on the right track. Money. People murder for money.

I think about Derek's burial place. I wonder if it wouldn't have been better to hide him in the farm land. So much less chance of discovery. Or is it? I look up at the fields and trees in the sloping acres ahead. And then, in my mind, I see bulldozers. Burying someone where there will be digging is no good. What are the chances anyone would ever dig up a trail in the woods? What are the chances a hand would emerge from the hillside next to the trail?

I stand. It's turning dark now and I'm heading home. I don't want to think about this anymore. Derek is gone so who will win the land now? I think I know the answer.

-25-

Copses of trees

Today, after a brief morning phone call, Sarah Jane and I go to the cafe for coffee. The park is a perfect place to meet since Sarah Jane doesn't have to drive too far. The air is cold. I love this time of year, but of course, before too long, the weather will deteriorate. I wonder what the staff does in the winter. Are they here? Do they close the place? No, I think there is a small weight room and I suppose people still hike or cross country ski. And I saw a paddle tennis court which should be open in the winter. I bet Larry is busy fixing up equipment and doing winter maintenance.

I see Sarah Jane approaching. She has donned classic khaki hiking togs and I think her boots look new.

"Been shopping?" I ask.

"Oh yes. At REI. My husband and I went there last night and cleared the clothes racks of outdoor apparel. It was a delight, trying on shorts and boots and warm flannel shirts. We were there so long that we closed the shop. Do you like it?" She twirls.

"I approve," I announce. "Shall we get that coffee and then take off?"

"Perfect," she answers. "I was looking at the map last night. I'm getting better at reading it and, in fact, bought this magnifier to be able to read the small print better." She turns and pulls her backpack off her shoulders, opens it, and extracts the glass.

"Really useful!" she exclaims. "I was noticing this small area near this building. It says 'Pavilion'. Do you know what that is?"

"I think I heard from someone – Simone, John, at the memorial service? Anyway not sure where, but I heard that Derek had a sort of social outdoor place in the park. Where he hosted sessions for various environmental causes. He was trying to preserve some land adjacent to the park and he was at odds with some developers. I guess he was trying to wield influence and gain people on his side of the question of what happens to a big farm nearby. It's for sale and there is quite a struggle about who develops it. I think the guy who is invested in Robert's, my son's, restaurant has a hand in the development. From what he has told me the idea is mixed housing and upscale services like restaurants and shops. But Derek hated the idea. He wanted to add the land to the park."

"That's interesting. I've seen the farm. Lovely. Rolling hills. Copses of trees."

"Yep, he was a man with a mission."

Sarah Jane points to the map she has laid out on the counter as I beckon to Tory for a couple of coffees. "Let's go down by the beech trees and see if we can find it." Sarah Jane looks up from her map with enthusiasm.

"OK. Fine by me. Here come the coffees."

Tory somewhat slams them on the table. Sarah Jane and I look at each other and each take a long draw on the brown liquid.

"Hmmm," we say in unison.

We decide to take a table where Sarah Jane regales me with stories of the annual church fete in her village at home, and after much laughing, we hoist our packs and start off.

We pass along the edge of the beech trees on Old Farm Road. The bark on the trees, so smooth and gray, seems to shine in the sun. I hear my stomach growl and remember the sesame sticks I popped into my bag. Stopping and removing my pack, I fish for the sticks. Sarah Jane pauses with me, looking curiously at my movements. I produce a plastic container and I take off the fitted top with much difficulty. I offer the treat to Sarah Jane. When she puts her hand into the container to get some crunchy sticks, it stops short against a plastic film. I look at her confused expression. "To have a sesame stick, apparently you have to fight for it." I peel back the film, freeing it from the container and immediately the wind blows it out of my hand and up the trail.

"Wait right there," I call as I take off after the film. When I bend to retrieve the film, it flies away again. Dragging my backpack, I hop from spot to spot where the film briefly alights until, in a large up swoosh of a wind gust, it flies up and off the trail. I hear Sarah Jane tittering behind me. I am hoping she's not videoing this to post online. Continuing my battle, I take off again and snag the bit of plastic. I clutch it and jam it into my pack. "You're mine," I declare. Sarah Jane laughs loudly and sputters out, "Small victories!"

Turning my head to put my pack on, I take in my location. From this spot I see what looks like another trail, more narrow and less defined, leaving the main artery to the left and a bit ahead of me. I look to the right and I can see that this faint trail continues over the main trail and down toward what I think would be the direction of the administration building. "Have we found a hidden trail?" I ask, feeling quite victorious after my plastic film defeat, and we take off on the small trail.

The trail is fairly easy to follow. I can see someone has been on it recently. We walk for about five or six minutes, up a rise and down, through a couple of clearings and back into the woods, sharing the sesame sticks as we go. This is fun. Exploring an unmarked trail while enjoying a snack and a new friend. The sun is bright and the breeze is pleasant.

I am surprised when I hear voices. And a car door slamming. I turn to Sarah Jane and her head is cocked, listening. We take about fifty steps and are standing at the end of the trail at the edge of a driveway. Two people have just gone into the house – a woman and man. Shrugging, I decide to try to figure out where I am. I head down the driveway, which is long, and finally come to a narrow road. This is not the pavilion.

"What do we do now?' Sarah Jane wonders. "We don't know where this road goes and we don't want to get lost. But can we just stroll up a stranger's driveway? I thought we were heading for the pavilion."

I look around and notice a mailbox. It has a number on it and a name. "343 Remy".

"Remy?" I exclaim pointing and motioning to Sarah Jane. "Like Derek?" Now I am curious.

"Are you up for nosing around a bit?" I ask Sarah Jane. "I think this is Derek Remy's place, you know, the murdered man. I mean, what are the chances of another Remy so close to the park with direct trail access. We have to check this out."

Sarah Jane looks at me for a moment, pondering my idea. Then she gets a sly smile and says, "I could use a wee adventure." I walk up the road a bit until I'm past the house and, in what I think is a smart maneuver, head up the hill on the other side toward the house, fighting my way through undergrowth. Sarah Jane follows. I feel sure our approach will be camouflaged by the woods.

After walking uphill parallel to the driveway, we stop to look around and get our bearings. I am surprised at what we see. I didn't realize that the lawn on this side of the house dropped steeply down a slope into the woods so that now we are at least twelve feet below the house. I motion uphill to Sarah Jane and we take off up the hill.

The grass is a bit slippery from rain or dew and our footing is difficult. Sarah Jane whispers loudly, "I can't make it. I'm falling and my boots are hurting."

I nod and motion for her to stay there. I go on and make it to the top. With little thought as to the fact I am trespassing, I sidle up to the house and look into a window. I am looking into an empty bedroom. I move around to the front of the house and stop abruptly when I see the two people inside. I hear a pop. They are popping open a bottle. They gaily tap glasses and smile at each other. And then I recognize Dale. Is he drinking champagne? This early in the day? And there is a young woman with whom he has locked elbows. They are both tossing back the bubbly. Who is the woman? I hear voices but I can't make out what they're saying. I crouch under the window to get closer. And out of nowhere I am knocked over and a wet furry nose pokes into my left ear. I shriek involuntarily. I crawl and roll awkwardly over to the side of the house to the top of the slope. The dog is barking now and the front door has opened. "Rocky!" I hear someone yell. "What is it?" On cue, I slide precariously down the slope into the woods, bumping my head on a tree trunk at the bottom. I sit up, dazed. I actually see stars. When I look around, Sarah Jane seems to have vanished. I look up and there, peering over the edge of the slope is the couple from the house – Dale and his co-celebrator. I jump to my feet and run back down the driveway. I think I hear Sarah Jane's boots behind me. As we race for the trail I am distracted by a door opening in a small shed on the edge of the property. I see a foot emerging, but before I can tell who it is, Dale and friend move across the front yard to look our way. I motion to Sarah Jane, who is also staring at the shed, and we escape into the woods and onto the trail. I run for a couple of minutes, and then, hearing only Sarah Jane's footsteps behind me, I sit down against a tree. Sarah Jane plops down beside me and immediately begins to remove a boot. I pant, "Did you see that person coming out of the little shed? Was he wearing camo? I could only see the lower part of one leg."

"I think maybe he was! Your camo man! What was he doing there?"

"I have no idea but I'm very confused. Is he with Dale? Does Dale know him?" I put my head in my hands." Oh no. Do you think they saw my face?" I gasp. "Dale might recognize me."

"Yes, they saw your face. I saw looks of surprise and then anger. That's why I moved further into the woods."

'Uh oh. This is bad. I shouldn't have been snooping so close to the house. But I was excited to find out where Derek lived and I didn't think I'd be seen. And popping champagne! What can that mean? And then, the man coming out of the shed. It's like Dale was purposely scaring us off."

Sarah Jane gives me an odd look. "Frankly, I think you need to calm down. You're jumping to all kinds of conclusions. I just saw a person peering into someone's private home and the occupants coming out to see who it was. And maybe the person at the shed was merely doing work around the place. Let's think carefully. And let's get back onto public land." She rubs her foot and I can see there is red along the side of her toes. We rest a few minutes and then get up to return back into the park. Maybe Sarah Jane is right. Maybe I am jumping to conclusions.

"Where is that Pavilion area?" Sarah Jane asks. "We had to have passed right by it."

"Maybe it is blocked by the trees. Let's go through the woods to the right here and see if we run into it. It has to be here."

I wait while Sarah Jane ties her boot back onto her foot. And then we push aside tree branches and tramp over roots until we get to the clearing. We emerge into a circle of stone seats. Sarah Jane and I look at each other. There is a pit in the middle for a fire and a tiny trail leads off from the center of it to the left of where we emerged. She points up and I see small lights in the trees.

"So this is Derek's outdoor space," I announce. "Very nice. Very rustic."

Sarah Jane walks forward until she is across the stone circle and out of view. I sit on a rock and wait. She is limping in her new boots and it takes her a while to return.

"Easy access to a small parking lot up there. And it comes off a road that, I think, could be the one the house was on. And it is adjacent to the Administration building – behind it with a walkway from the main lot."

"How convenient," I say. "Derek had a quick walk from his house to the Pavilion."

"This is like finding a secret garden," Sarah Jane adds, with a smile. "Pretty cool."

We sit on the stones a while, glancing about.

"You want to head back to the cars or do you want to hike on?" I question.

"I need to get out of these boots," she says sadly. "Let's go back up to that little parking lot and then walk up through the main lot to the cars. I can move along without these boots when we get to the paved part."

"Maybe you can return the boots," I suggest.

Sarah Jane and I look at them and we see they are muddy and scratched.

"Maybe they would fit me," I add, hoping to find a way to encourage Sarah Jane.

"Do you wear a size 8?" she asks.

"No, er, maybe with a lot of socks."

I give her a hug and a smile. I leave her to get out of the boots and head to Bunny Hill. I want to spend more time in the park.

-26-

Bearded man in khaki

Climbing up Bunny Hill always makes me feel good. That's why I come here a lot. It's too early to head home and I want to take in the lovely view down to the meadow. There never seems to be anyone there. I suppose the steep incline puts people off. I get to the top, breathing hard, and sit on a stump. The wind is up and I cuddle into my coat. I look upward to see the boughs waving in the wind. I gaze back over the fields. I think about the past few days. I don't want to know that administrative duo/trio. I want to be just another, anonymous visitor instead of the ire-producing body finder. I contemplate. It seems to me that John and Margot are two people who prefer to do their jobs in relative isolation, probably because encounters with the public are mostly complaints. I get that. It's an easier job when they don't have to deal with suggestions from visitors or call the police in. I've made their lives harder. I should have understood that. And I don't want to know anything about camo man. I want to forget ever seeing him by the creek or exiting a shed.

As I look over the meadow far down the vista, I see the man in a utility vehicle, slowly winding down a trail. There's a good chance that's Larry. He's dressed in khaki with a large brimmed hat. He is small from my vantage point and I can't see his face well but I think I see a beard. A beard! Can't be Larry. Simone said he had no beard, but there is definitely something below this guy's mouth and on his chin. Could he be my rescuer on the rock? Does he work here too? But Simone never talked about another employee.

I keep an eye on the khaki guy's progress. So there is Larry who I haven't properly seen, guy with beard who apparently works here and rescued me and ran away and might have been in a shed on Derek's property and is now tooling about the park in a work vehicle, and then, I can't forget him, there's the guy I heard laughing in the woods. Simone needs to know there may be another employee with a beard.

I refocus on the bearded man in khaki. He winds through the meadow, stopping occasionally to fuss with something – a bit of trash, a wayward plant, something dead – then wanders out of my sight and I sit for a while. It's so pleasant here. Determined to turn my mind from the men in the park, I lay back and look up into the dancing tree tops. I'm too suspicious, I think. That comes from finding a body and hanging out with a detective.

With my eyes closed, I enjoy the air on my face. I can feel sleep coming so I rise to my feet to avoid finding myself jarred awake in the dark. My foot steps on something. It cracks like plastic. When I look down, I see it's a cell phone. Really, a second cell phone? It looks a lot like the last one – same model in a black case. Do I tromp back into John's office with it? No, I need to make myself scarce there and besides, I really crushed it. I'm sure it's not usable. Tucking it into my pocket, I head down the hill.

-27-

Red gingham

My phone rings. It's Robert. "Hi there. How are you?"

"Good, Mom. Say, I was thinking of stopping by this evening and grilling up a few things. OK by you?"

"Sure, will there be anything for me to eat?"

"Yep, I'll make you dinner."

"Need me to go to the store?"

"Nope, I'll do the shopping."

"Hey, I was thinking of asking Sarah Jane, my British friend, over sometime. I met her in Rob Ryan Park and she's delightful. She might enjoy a meal made by my famous griller of a son. Can I invite her and her husband? Gee, I'm not sure of his name, maybe John?"

"Sure. Add a bit of international flair. I'll be there before six."

"See you then. I'm looking forward to this!"

I find Sarah Jane in my contacts and ring her. "Hi, it's Kate. Are you interested in coming here for dinner tonight. I know it's short notice but ..."

"Where are you?"

"I'm home. I thought you and your husband could come

over. Robert, my son, is grilling on the patio. I'll grab some wine and we can make the most of this warm evening in October."

"It's sounds nice but John is out tonight, so it's just me. And I'm not sure how far away you are or how hard it would be for me to drive there." Her voice trails off.

"Why don't I come and get you? We can stop for wine and, after dinner, someone will get you home."

"That's seems a lot of trouble."

"Of course it isn't. It's not that far to your hotel. Robert is bringing the food so I have lots of time. Let's see, it's 3:00 now. I'll come by around four."

"Well, OK!" Sarah Jane replies. "I'll be ready."

"A little party," I think. "I really would have loved to have met John."

I run around the house, clearing away some clutter. Then I go out to the deck and patio and clean off the glass on the tables and wipe away any spots on the chairs. I change my clothes and head to the car.

When I pull into the hotel lot, Sarah Jane is waiting. She is in a denim dress and red shoes and a long sweater, er, jumper as she would call it.

"You look so pretty!" I say. "This will be a fancy party."

She blushes bright red as she gets into the car. "Did I overdo it?"

"No, not at all." I give her a big smile. She really has become a good friend in the short time I have known her. I'm lucky to have a few young people for friends.

"OK, let's get some wine and maybe a couple of beers. Is wine OK for you?"

"Oh yes. Lovely."

"And, I was thinking, Robert said he would bring the food but I know he won't bring dessert. Let's pick up something for after dinner."

Sarah Jane touches my arm and exclaims, "Would you like me to make something? I love to bake!"

"Oh, sure. Do you have something in mind?"

"Well, I have a small repertoire that I know from memory. Let's see. How about a Victoria Sponge? It's simple and quick."

"Really?" I ask. "That sounds sophisticated. You don't have to go to a lot of trouble."

"No trouble. It's simple, really. I make them all the time for church events. My husband loves a Victoria Sponge."

"Well, then." I turn to smile at her. "Let's have at it. What do we need to pick up for ingredients?"

"Okay, let me think. Do you have eggs? Flour and sugar? Butter?"

"Yes, yes, and yes. What else?"

"Two baking tins. Some good jam."

"No jam. Certainly no good jam."

"Can we manage to secure some?"

"Yes we can," I say as I turn into the shopping center.

After grabbing wine at the liquor store, we head into the Giant Eagle. Sarah Jane balks a bit at the name. "I know," I say. "It's a ubiquitous grocery around here. But they should have beer and jam."

I leave Sarah Jane at the jam and jelly aisle and dash over to get a couple of six packs. When I get back, she is still reading labels from jam jars.

"No good?" I ask.

"Just fine. Different than what I'm used to at home but," she gently selects a glass jar with a red gingham top, "I recognize this Bonne Maman. And, I almost forgot, whipping cream."

We go to the dairy section and she grabs a pint of heavy cream.

"You're going to whip that yourself?" I ask tentatively.

"Of course," is her quick reply.

When we get into the house, Sarah Jane makes lovely murmurings about my home, and then she exclaims, "We need to get the butter out!"

"Oh, you don't want it to be cold?"

"No, room temperature is necessary."

I retrieve the butter and then pull out the flour, sugar, measuring cups, a bowl and two cake pans.

"What else do you need?"

"Eggs – you can get those out now too. Oh, and I forgot. Baking powder. A mixer. And the scale. And then I think we're all set."

"Scale? What do you mean by scale?"

"To measure. You know, the flour and sugar and butter."

I point to the measuring cups. "Can't you use these?'

She stares. "I only know the recipe with measurement in grams."

I see she is distressed. Apparently a lack of a kitchen scale is about to derail the whole dessert.

"Well, how about…. Target!"

"Target?" She looks at me as if I am babbling foolishly.

"Yeah. We can run to Target while that butter warms up. I bet they sell scales."

Sarah Jane follows me to the car and we drive the couple of miles to the Target store. We rove around until we come to the kitchen gadgets aisle and there it is, a scale. Sarah Jane picks it up and hugs it to her breast. I grab it from her and say, "my treat" while checking the price. A twelve dollar scale has saved the day. I didn't want Sarah Jane to be disappointed and I truly didn't want to miss out on her Victoria sponge.

When we pull into the drive I see that Robert has beat us here. He's in the kitchen, humming and forming burgers.

"Hey, you're earlier than I expected. Meet Sarah Jane Pratt. My son Robert. I open my palms to each and look back and forth.

"I didn't know you have such a handsome son, Kate. Lovely to meet you."

Roberts smiles and takes her hands, giving her a light kiss on the back of one hand. He looks up at me. "The closest thing to royalty we have here, Mom."

Sarah Jane is tickled.

"And we have a treat ahead. Sarah Jane is making us a Victoria sponge."

"Oh wow! Really?"

I hold up the scale. "We were at Target getting a scale. An English baker needs her scale."

"If only I'd known, Mom, I have one of those in my apartment."

"Well now I have one too." I am feeling so happy with my son and friend here.

Sarah Jane is looking at the oven controls. "What would 180 C be on this?"

I grab my tablet and Google for the conversion. "You want 356 on that oven."

She smiles and expertly sets the temperature.

I pour myself a glass of wine and watch my cooks. Robert is slicing vegetables and Sarah Jane has torn right into the scale package. Carefully measuring on the scale, Sarah Jane breaks the eggs into the bowl, followed by the butter, flour, and sugar. She gives me a quizzical look as she picks up the baking powder. I jump up and fetch the measuring spoons. In goes the last ingredient.

I sip wine while the mixer whirs. Soon the pans are buttered and the batter is poured. Sarah Jane weighs each pan to see they are evenly filled and pops them into the oven. "That scale is useful," I think.

The vegetables are ready to put on the grill in their cast iron pan. We all file out and relax. Robert has lit the chiminea and we huddle around it. Sarah Jane and Robert are bantering about Hadrian's Wall. I look up at the blue sky. And then, out of nowhere, Simone rounds the house. "I thought I smelled Robert at a grill." She plops into a wicker chair next to Robert, holding her hands out to the chiminea. A timer goes off and Sarah Jane heads to the kitchen. I follow like a puppy.

After Sarah Jane removes the cake from the oven and has it cooling on a rack, I decide to do a pre-cleanup of the kitchen before we eat. The high window in the back of the kitchen is open, and below it sits Robert and Simone. I can see Sarah Jane at the edge of the yard, admiring the last remnants of the neighbors' large perennial garden.

"So how is this case shaping up?" Robert asks Simone.

I pause in my cleaning. I want to hear this.

"The dead fellow had some interesting relationships with a few folks. A brother and a brother-in-law who had animosity toward him. For different issues. And both are in from out of town. That gives us all pause down in the incident room. Then there is a cadre of land developers that were competing with Derek for a prime piece of property. I mean he was generous to a fault with money if he wanted to be. He loved the park and wanted to expand it. He had a lot of supporters."

"Sounds like a tricky guy to define. Must make it harder to find a motive."

"Like I said, there is the family angle. We're been tracing their past movements."

"And Mom said he was strangled or hung. There was some kind of mark on his neck?

"Yep, a rope burn. But he was hit with a piece of wood on the skull. That's what did him in. That's what the coroner has determined."

She paused for a breath. "So that's it. More than I should say but this house seems to turn me into a blabber mouth. Luckily you and Kate can keep your mouths shut."

She stops. I hear Robert laugh. "I didn't hear a thing."

"Oh, tell me about the restaurant. Can't wait to party there."

I was enjoying this conversation. The open window was a great blind. I could see why Simone enjoyed overhearing Junie's talk with me a few day earlier.

"What were you doing in the neighborhood," Roberts asks. "Were you at Junie and Angus's?

"You always were an observant one," Simone replies fondly to Robert. "Yep, I overheard Junie telling your mother about his relationship with Derek..."

"Junie knew Derek?"

"Yup, go figure. Junie and Derek were in a grief counseling group together. And they had a couple of drinks together a few times."

"So what did you want to know?"

"Well, I confessed to Junie that I had eavesdropped on him from the upstairs window and he clarified a couple of things. I may ask him to make a formal statement about a couple of conversations he had with Derek, just to get them on the record."

"Mom is, of course, obsessed with hiking at the park. She is drawn to a mystery like a squirrel to an acorn. I wish she wasn't. She seems to have insulted the park employees. What's up with that?"

"They're a tight knit, altogether mediocre group. It seems that when she came in and demanded to report a crime and was dropping mud about, she made a bad impression. They knew Derek, of course. He hired them for tasks he needed done – extra work when he had his evening events. When I spoke with them I found them cooperative and pleasant."

"Ha!" The word escapes my lips before I stop it.

"What's that?" Simone says, rising from her chair and looking through the window at me. "Speaking of eavesdropping."

-28-

English cake

The assembly of the cake begins. I watch as Sarah Jane carefully spreads the 'good' jam and begins whipping the cream. Then she takes the cream and loads it into a plastic bag where she has lopped off a corner. She raises on her tiptoes and, with tongue out moving along her lips in concentration, begins piping a pattern on the top of the cake. Leaning in but trying not to get my nose too far into the procedures, I watch my artistic friend create a lattice on the cake. It is beautiful. I turn to stare at her. I'm awestruck. But she carries on, the tip of the plastic bag moving in a mesmerizing motion. With a quick shift, she takes the bag to her lips and sucks out a bit of cream.

"My favorite part of piping!" she exclaims.

As I continue to stare in admiration, she takes an ordinary kitchen spoon and dips it into the jam. Again, her head bends in concentration as she begins decorating. The sponge is topped with a rosebud center! Sarah Jane stands back smiling as she looks over her work. Bowing her head, she parades it out the back door to the patio table. I follow with forks and plates. I'm not sure Sarah Jane was prepared for the appreciation shown by the Americans. Robert quietly shakes her hand while beaming at the cake. Simone emits a breathless 'Aah!' Sarah Jane blushes pink and then red until she is the same color as the jam. And then we all applaud.

I sniff the air. There is smoke coming from under the grill lid. "May I make a suggestion? It smells like meat out here and it's getting cloudy. Let's bundle up and have dessert on the front porch. I'll just grab the sponge and the utensils and set it up on the table out there. Robert, when you are ready, we can all congregate there."

Everyone nods and I head to the porch. The cake looks lovely sitting on the little table by the door. If the mail carrier was due, he might be tempted to take a piece, or the whole thing, and I wouldn't be able to blame him. I head back to the deck.

"All ready?"

It's obvious I have come into the middle of a conversation. It's very quiet and everyone is looking at me. "What's going on?" I ask. "Is something wrong?"

Simone, Robert, and Sarah Jane look at each other. Sarah Jane turns to me and shrugs. I focus on each of them in turn until Robert blurts out, "Mom, and Sarah Jane, shouldn't you avoid that park for a bit? They're still solving the death," he points to Simone.

Sarah Jane starts, "It's my entertainment, Robert. It's lovely there. I do avoid that path well, er, you know, but there is a lovely cafe and..." She trails off. I pick up the thread, "We have found a mutual pleasure in walking in the park. And we do enjoy the cafe. And, we are amused by the fact that we can hear the office people talking when we are in the Ladies Room." Sarah Jane and I smile at each other.

"Hear them talking?" Simone picks up on this.

"Yep. Sounds go through the wall in the last stall. Little jabs at each other. It seems it is not a convivial office. And if Margot looks up from her counter when I leave the bathroom, she glares at me. I do my best to be friendly but, I sort of..."

"Spilled your tea all over her paperwork?" Simone interjects. Robert puts his head in his hands.

"They can be a bit unfriendly," chimes in Sarah Jane. "When I first discovered the park I went into the building and there was Margot – I didn't know her name at the time – and I marched right up to her to ask for a map. She pointed to the rack just inside the door. Then she said, 'You sound funny.'

It took me a moment to realize that she meant my accent. So I said, 'Well, I'm from England. It's nice to meet you. My name is Sarah Jane Pratt.' She repeated my name, spitting out the Pratt as if it was a curse and then she turned on her heel and walked into the office. I was put off, I can tell you."

Robert and Simone look at each other. Simone sighs, "OK. OK. I'll find some excuse to go back in and talk with them. I think I'm getting the vibe now."

With a small sense of victory, I extend my arm to the front of the house. "Dessert is served!"

Sarah Jane is the first to enter the porch. "Where's the sponge?" she ask.

I follow behind. "Just there, on the little table..." But it's not there.

I can hear Robert and Simone laughing as they try to enter the porch but I am blocking the door.

"Move aside, lady," Roberts calls. "I want to taste some of this English cake."

I point to the table. "It's gone." Sarah Jane looks at us pleadingly.

"Where?" is all Robert can come up with.

"I don't know." I look around the porch. "I hope it wasn't the squirrels. Sometimes they think they own this porch. I can't believe it."

"It wasn't squirrels", says Simone. "They couldn't have lifted it so neatly."

I look. No crumbs left behind. No disheveled silverware.

"You're right, detective. Then who could it have been?"

Simone pushes to the top of the stairs and looks up and down the street. "No idea."

Robert chimes in. "There is a gremlin next door, you know." He points to the house up the street. I know he means Freddie. He and Freddie were arch rivals over the chiminea, although to be fair, Freddie can't be more than ten years old.

As I glance over at Sarah Jane, I see tears are forming in her blue eyes. One giant drop escapes and runs slowly down her cheek. I follow its path to her chin where it falls off and plops onto one of her red shoes. I put my arm around her shoulders until she wipes her eyes and gives a weak smile.

"Are you okay now?" I hate that her triumph has turned into sadness.

"Yes, er, maybe. I think I want to go home now."

Simone and Robert, have begun to stack the dessert plates and forks. We all slowly traipse back into the house, my arm still around Sarah Jane. As she enters the dining room on her way to the kitchen, Sarah Jane is caught up short.

"What's this?" she points at my crime board. She leans in. Robert sees her and does the same.

Simone answers first. "Don't you two know a crime board when you see one? Part of the basic police technique when solving a crime."

Sarah Jane's mouth drops open. "You have it here? This is your headquarters?"

Robert laughs. "If my tax money is going to a police unit that put this Crime Board together, I'm going to complain to someone."

I turn to Sarah Jane. "Just me playing around with ideas." I give Robert an exasperated look. "Let's take you home now, Sarah Jane. You look tired."

Sarah Jane nods and grabs her pocket book.

Robert's Story 09

I leave Mom's and the missing sponge cake and the dining room crime board. I see lights on in the bistro so I pull into a spot and let myself in. Bobby and Sebastian are moving tables around.

"What's this?" I ask, curious as to why they are rearranging.

"Sebastian was gazing over the bar and decided we could, perhaps, get in one more table if we moved the furniture a bit," Bobby tells me.

"And can you?" I ask.

"To be determined. At this point we've not sure where we started, so we can't be sure if the tables are actually just back where they started. What do you think?"

"Uh," I stammer as I look over the tables. The chairs are stacked in the booths along the walls. "The problem is, without the chairs under the tables, you really can't tell if there is enough room between tables. Aren't there guidelines for that?"

"Yea, we have the spacing in mind. The question is – is this better than before… or is it the same as before?"

I look to Sebastian. He looks done in.

"I think it looks different," I begin. "But I don't see where you will put an extra table."

Bobby grabs a chair from a booth and sits. Sebastian plops on a bar stool. They both stare at the floor.

Seeing their glum expressions, I decide I need to act so I begin moving the tables to where I think they used to be. Terence comes out of the kitchen.

"What's up?" he says. "I was putting away stock and I heard all the scraping."

"Just a bit of experimentation with table arrangement," I say as I reposition the table I just moved.

"I liked it the way it was," Terence says. "I thought it looked good."

"OK, genius." Bobby rises and points to the furniture. "Put it back the way it was."

Terence looks at him. "Me?"

"I'll help," I chime in. "Come grab the other side of this table."

I let Terence determine the direction we move. It's like allowing someone at a séance to push the Ouija piece. We keep moving tables until, my God, the room looks as it did this morning, I look at Bobby and Sebastian. They are gaping.

"How did you do that so easily?" Bobby asks.

"The tables aren't heavy," Terence says. "What a bunch of wusses," he calls back as he goes back into the kitchen.

"He's a magician!" Sebastian exclaims. "You were just following along, right Robert?"

"Yep. He's a magician all right. There's magic all around. I just came from my Mom's where Simon and Sarah Jane – friend of Mom's from the park – and I were having dinner. Somehow we made a whole cake disappear."

"Funny. I wish you'd saved some for us."

"No, we didn't eat it. It was on the porch and when we went out to eat it, it was gone! Disappeared."

"Who ate it?" Bobby asks.

"Whoever stole it I guess."

"An animal?" Sebastian screws up his face.

"No, carefully carried off. Not a crumb left behind."

"You mean someone walked up and took it?"

"Yep. That is what I mean," I say somewhat formally.

"And what did the detective say?" Sebastian queried.

"Not her job to find missing cake."

We all laugh. I see the kitchen door close gently. Terence eavesdropping, I think.

"So what did you do then?"

"Well, we filed back into the house and Sarah Jane noticed Mom's Crime Board. That was a hoot."

"Crime board?"

"Yes, since she found that body she has appointed herself, again I might say, amateur sleuth. So she made a board of all the particulars in the case. She scrounged the internet for photos and did some alterations on some of them to complete the board. Totally ridiculous."

"Who's on this board?"

"The dead guy's picture is there. And his dead wife's is there too, although I'm not sure why. And then there are the suspects."

"And they are..."

"The usual suspects ... the brother who will inherit, the brother-in-law who always hated the dead guy, some woman who thought she was getting money from the dead wife but it was withheld by the dead guy, some people the dead guy was going up against to buy a big farm next to the park. Dead guy wanted to add the land to the park – preserve it you know, but the developer guys want to make a pile of money from the land."

"Wow. No wonder the guy's dead with all those enemies." Sebastian rubs his chin.

"Hang on," Bobby interjects. "What farm was this they were arguing over? I mean it has to be that big one off Route 8. What else abuts the park?"

"That's it," I answer.

"Oh boy," Bobby says looking at Sebastian. "Remember Jim, our investor extraordinaire, talking over a project like that? He was going to develop a shopping/dining area in a new community. And he was bitching that the purchase of the land was held up by some idiot. At least that's what he called him."

"I thought Jim Tucci might be in on this." I lament.

"Yep. Big Jim and his big mouth. He was spouting on about it a couple of weeks ago. Come to think of it, he hasn't mentioned it lately."

"OMG! He might be a suspect. He might be a prime suspect!" Sebastian looks from me to Bobby.

"Well, not sure about that. Could be one of many. My mom has it in for the park workers. And, well maybe Sarah Jane because she's a bit under her influence. I mean, the woman at the counter there is suspect because when Sarah Jane said something to her the woman said, 'You talk funny.' Oh, Sarah Jane is British."

Sebastian and Bobby can only stare at me.

"There's all kind of crazy going on. Whatever you do, if my mother comes in here, don't mention the crime."

-29-

Feeling devilish

The phone rings. It's Sarah Jane.

"Hey, Sarah Jane. Have you gotten over your lost cake? I can't imagine what happened to it and I'm sorry, again. What's up?"

"I'm headed back over to the park later for an adventure. I can't sit around here so I'm making a lunch and you could come along. We have a frig at the hotel where I keep lunch food. I thought I'd take my lunch to Inspiration Point and have a jolly sit down and listen to the wind in the trees. Lovely today. Will you meet me?"

"Nope. But it's a very nice offer. I need to be here to pay my mower and run an errand or two. Inspiration Point," I repeat. "I've been by there. Didn't see anything that inspiring about it, just a small bluff overlooking more woods below."

"It's calm there," she said. "At breakfast my husband let drop that we are staying on a bit because he has an opportunity to participate in some church or other, so I am using the time to meditate on my life. Frankly, I was feeling a bit homesick and I need a change of mood. Are you sure you don't want to come with me? I could share what bit I have in the satchel."

"While you work on your mood change, I'm needed here. As I said. Things to do. A nap to take. Such is my busy life."

Sarah Jane chuckles.

"Have you ever seen the maintenance guy over there? A Larry Cloud?"

"Cloud? No, don't know him."

"I think I saw him on a mower or some contraption when I was on Bunny Hill. He was way below though. Just wondered if you could describe him. He was wearing khakis."

"No, I mean I may have seen some worker here or there. Did I tell you John and I went over to the park together last night and had the most lovely walk and saw the sun setting over the creek and, well, it was romantic."

I can almost feel her blushing.

Sarah Jane continues. "But, oh wait, Larry. Yes, I heard his name last night. Once again I ended up in the dreaded last bathroom stall and once again I heard something I didn't want to. I heard Margo say, 'Larry, did you lose another one? And did you get that downed tree moved?' to which I think Larry replied something like 'Stop bossing me around.' I really have no interest in the machinations in that office."

"Pick another stall," I suggest.

"Well it was busy in there. I think that cafe is filling people up with tea and coffee and it is placing a burden on the three stall restroom. Anyway, I ran into a guy, I think in a tan shirt, coming out of the office as I left the girls' loo and couldn't resist saying,' I heard there is a tree down' – I was feeling devilish. He gave me a look and headed back into the office. That must have been Larry. How could I forget?"

"Did he have a beard?"

"No, no beard. At least I don't remember one."

"I've never seen Larry up close. I guess he's the man riding around the park on a maintenance vehicle, but he's always at a distance with a hat over his head. I don't know why I expected a beard."

"Hmm. But, let me continue to describe my encounter in the office last night. It was quite the scene. So park map in hand, I look over to the counter in the foyer and since Margot is not there and it's clear of papers. I open the park map and spread it out on the surface. Once again, not meaning to listen in on other people's conversation, I find myself overhearing Larry and Margot. These people are indiscreet! I mean this is a public building. I'm not trespassing."

"So, tell me, what did you hear?" I'm all ears. Margot, Larry, and John amuse me while at the same time annoy me. They are the local three stooges.

"Margot is scolding Larry – like a schoolboy – saying 'behave yourself and keep in touch. I can't keep covering for you forever.'"

"After I fell in the creek, it took John two communication methods to get hold of Larry. Apparently he goes AWOL during work hours."

"Well, not sure, but then Margot says, rather loudly, 'You have a job to do. I'm heading to my car and you should get at it before I get back.'"

"Wow. Had no idea Margot ordered Larry around."

"And then Margot rushes out of the office, sees me hanging over her counter and gets an odd look on her face. I know that she knows I heard her. And I know that she knows that I know that. So I nonchalantly fold up the map and give her a smile and head to the door. And then, despite her announcement that she is heading to her car, she storms back into the office and slams the door. The whole building shook. But before I can get out the door, a man with very white, full hair – rather handsome for an older man, although his shirt was buttoned wrong – ruined the effect – comes up and stops me. He latches onto my arm and says, 'You know the woman who found the body, don't you?' And I say, 'Maybe.' I was taken aback. He goes on. 'She seems to be everywhere in this park. I'd stay away from her.' So then John Logan comes up and pulls me away from and gives this guy hard look. He was quite gallant."

"Huh?" I bark. "What have I… Oh wait. Good looking man with bouffant white hair in his fifties? I bet that was Dale, the dead man's brother. You didn't recognize him?"

"Why would I?"

"I saw him at Derek's memorial service. Then he was in Derek's house, you know, on our house-peeking episode."

"Oh, OK, let me go on. But before John pulls me out the door I announce, 'She has been a good friend to me since I've been in America and we have become dear chums. She tells me all about this park.' I'm beginning to have your trepidation about that building."

Sarah Jane gives a big sigh. "I'm off to go hiking and eat my food. The ins and outs of office politics is none of my business even though they insist on blabbing it about the building. And I don't appreciate a stranger grabbing my arm and telling me who I can and cannot see."

I bid the feisty Sarah Jane goodbye. I can almost hear her stomping over to the Old Road trailhead that will get her to Inspiration Point. She's plucky, I think. And very good at eavesdropping.

-30-

Came in kindness

I am reading an Iris Murdoch mystery and trying to get all the character names straight. She has a lot of them and I have to keep flipping back in the book to keep them straight. Just as I feel I have a grasp on them, I am startled by someone walking up my porch stairs. I look up to see a man with white hair, in his fifties and honestly for a moment I'm sure that Derek has reappeared. I drop the book and rise in my chair, moving toward the door.

"You're Dale?" I question, slowly backing up. Has he come to tell me to stay away from Sarah Jane? What is he up to?

"Oh, sorry. I didn't mean to upset you. In fact, I came here to see how you are."

"But we don't really know each other..." I pause. I am entirely uncomfortable with the situation and I don't want to bring up Derek's name. I'm afraid my snooping has brought him to my front door. Where's Simone? I should have listened to her.

"I get that but you know I'm Dale. Derek's brother. You were at the memorial and you know I know that you found the body. And I saw you and that English girl outside Derek's house. You are traumatized by finding the body, right? I have been haunted by how horrible that must have been and I decided to, well, again thank you for finding him and also reiterate that I'm sorry you had to go through that experience."

"You didn't have anything to do with all that, did you?" I now have my hand on the door knob. "And why did you tell Sarah Jane to avoid me? What are you worried about? And I am having trouble believing that you have any concern for me at all."

"Please, don't be alarmed. I'm here with the best of intentions. With Derek dying in that park and the police about and you sneaking up to the house, I just thought that young woman with the lovely English accent should be careful. No one knows who to trust and she seems very trusting. And I'm upset about your experience in finding the body. Truly."

"How did you even know where I live?" I question.

"I was talking to Margot, she works at the park, and I was expressing my concerns and she said she had your address. She was a bit reluctant, very protective of you, but I have to admit I cajoled it out of her." He gives a slight shrug and his face turns sheepish.

"I think you should go," I say. "First, this is wrong – you coming to my home – and second, I don't believe for a minute that Margot would protect me."

"Why not?"

"She doesn't like me. She sort of hates me."

"Margot? But she has been nothing but kind about this whole thing. And she is worried about you."

"No, she's not. She found me messy and annoying, right from the start. She is giving you a line."

Dale looks confused. I'm not buying his kindness.

"Ok," he says finally. "Let me back down the steps into the yard so you don't feel threatened. I am sincere in my feelings, I assure you. I know there has been a lot of talk about me inheriting money. But you're misconstruing this."

"I saw you. I saw you and a woman at Derek's house. And you know I did and now you have asked Margot for my address and you're going to…."

"Yes, I am living at Derek's. I was there waiting for him to come home when I found about his death. I stayed with him often. And I didn't really ask Margot for your address, I just said I wanted to talk with you and she suddenly obliged."

"I'll bet she did. But, when I saw you and the woman, you seemed close, and frankly, like you were celebrating."

"That was Chloe from a school that Rhonda had agreed to fund. Chloe cornered me, not the first time, about the money promised to her, and, because I felt backed into a corner, I told her I would go along with Rhonda's wishes. Rhonda was Derek's wife and she had promised Chloe…"

"I know about that. So the woman you were drinking with was Chloe, from the school?"

"Yes. How do you know about the school and the funding?"

"I, um, I guessed. I guessed maybe Chloe and Rhonda were close…"

"That makes no sense."

And it doesn't. But I don't want to reveal how I know so I am desperately grasping for an explanation. Time to divert the topic, I think. This isn't going well.

"Well, anyway," I continue. "To my eyes you two seemed

happy about Derek's death and, well, here you are at my house and you can see why I'm rather nervous. In fact," I grab my phone from a side table on the porch, "I'm going to make a call."

"Go ahead. I don't want you to feel uncomfortable. I really came in kindness."

"In kindness?! But you warned Sarah Jane about me. And the fact is that you will inherit a lot of money. You're a suspect." I point at him as I say this. He steps back.

"I'm sure I am. But I didn't do it. And about Sarah Jane, well, I've observed her when I was at the park. As I said, she seems so innocent and trusting. And you were nosing around the house and then I saw her with you and I felt that maybe she should steer clear of this whole thing. I mean she is stepping into the middle of a murder investigation."

"OK, well then, the best thing you can do for sweet Sarah Jane is to solve the murder. Who did it?" I ask bluntly. "Who among you offed your brother?"

"My money's on Michael Sespin, Rhonda's brother."

I raise an eyebrow and put my hands on my hips in distaste.

"Ok, I'm sorry. That sounded bad." He looks at the ground. He does have a bit of a disheveled look and maybe even the appeal of a lost puppy. He seems so sad, and sort of harmless. I make a rash decision. If I invite him to the porch, I may get info. Yes, this will help Simone.

"Ok, come on up and take a seat. We're in full view of a number of dog walkers." I point to the street where a small woman is being dragged along the pavement by a large black dog. "What's your story?"

"Everything I said was true. I am in the amending business.

It comes from being in AA. You've heard of their tenet of making amendments?"

"I don't believe that. You were drinking champagne with Chloe."

"Sparkling water. Nothing more."

I stare at him. That hang dog look of his makes me warm to him. So is he really giving some of his money to Chloe? I'm confused.

"Tell me the whole story. Why are you here? What's the true deal with Chloe? What was your relationship with your brother?"

"Boy, you should work for the police. I can explain the interaction between me and Derek and Rhonda."

"OK, shoot."

"Derek and I had a troubled relationship, mostly due to my money problems. See, I wanted to make it big like Derek so I kept trying and losing and it was okay while Rhonda was alive. She was so supportive of me. She understood our background, Derek and mine, and she felt I could use a boost."

"What background?"

"It was a family thing. A father who blamed me for a sister who drowned. But I can't talk about that."

I look at Dale. Is this true? Or a melodramatic tale? I don't want to be a chump but then ...

"Anyway, it's a very sad but very old story and Rhonda knew it and she liked me and she had lots of her own money and she supported my ventures. Derek thought she was a fool, but he could be sort of, er, arrogant. Very pleased with himself. Although understandably. I think he was as confused as I was."

"Once Rhonda died, of course the money stopped. I was in debt. I needed help. So I would occasionally come here and make a plea to Derek. He would usually, reluctantly, give in so we made a plan to draw down the debt and get me on my feet. He was critical of me and made strict requirements. It was tough. Not that I didn't need structure but..."

"So anyway, I came by to review things with him, and he knew I was coming, but my arrival time was tentative so when I showed up and he wasn't there, I just moved into my normal room and waited for his return. I knew he wouldn't mind."

"And then you found out he was dead."

"Yes, it was awful. He's the only one I have left."

"And then Chloe?"

"Well she came by when she found out about the money and, she kept going on about Rhonda's intentions – she had correspondence to the effect. I was trying to decide what to do. Derek hated giving money away as much as Rhonda was generous."

"Do you think Derek killed Rhonda?"

"Heavens no! He loved her."

"Oh, okay. Go on."

"Well that's it. Now I find myself a prime suspect and no one talks to me except Chloe, and well, Margot a bit. John is friendly enough but standoffish."

"And Larry?"

"Who?"

"Never mind. So explain how you ended up on my porch."

"Well, I'm determined to stay here and wait for the release of the body and I got to thinking about this woman who I met at the memorial service who grabbed a dead hand and how awful that was and then I thought well, if she hadn't would Derek have been found? Or at least when would he have been found? And I thought I'd check in with you. I didn't remember your name or know your address."

"And Margot told you how to find me?" I remember I had to give my basic information to John when I reported the incident.

"She did. I asked the police but they wouldn't tell me so..."

"You told her you were coming here? Didn't she think that was odd? You seeking out the muddy woman who had found your brother's hand?"

"I didn't really tell her I was coming here. I just expressed concern for you. As she did."

"So, here you are."

"So here I am. And things aren't going as well as I had hoped."

"I'm feeling sorry for you Dale, but something tells me I need to keep you at arm's length. I can be too trusting. I have to tell the detective you've been here."

"Are you going to say you were being harassed?"

"No, but don't you think that as a suspect you should be careful whose porch you sit on?"

"Maybe."

We stare at each other for a minute or two and then he stands.

"I guess I better move on. This was impertinent, coming here unannounced. Thank you for hearing me out."

And then he gives me a cute salute and leaves. I notice he had parked his car up the street a bit. Should I be suspicious of that? Should I be suspicious at all? People tell me to be careful all the time but when I think about Dale, I decide he's okay.

-31-

An ambulance and a police car

I wake up with a start from a nap realizing I have been dreaming about the park office. The statements Sarah Jane told me have evoked a dream in which Margot and John and Larry are all sorting paper at the counter. Furiously. A multitude of paper. I'm going to tell Simone. Not about the dream but about what Sarah Jane overheard and about Dale's visit. I ring Simone but she's not in. I tell the officer who picks up at the station that I need her to call me. Or see me. He mumbles an okay and hangs up abruptly.

Because I feel so unsettled, I decide to call Sarah Jane and see how her lunch is going, or maybe how it went. I'm not sure I'll reach her while she's in the park, but I'll try. I touch her name in my phone and listen to it ringing. No luck. I sit down in my living room to think about it, but I can't settle. I don't want to stop by the restaurant because Robert doesn't want to hear about my sleuthing. I think for a while, weighing Sarah Jane's off-handedness about things and Robert's frustration at my investigating. I make tea. I eat a yogurt. I load the washer.

And then, because I can't ignore my impulse, I put on my hiking boots and get in my car to head back to the park, mostly because I hope to run into Sarah Jane. I want to tell her about my dream and talk again about what she heard. Although, as I remember her remark about not caring about what the park people are saying, I wonder if she will want to talk about it. Again I am letting those quarrelsome people get under my skin. It's just that I don't like not being liked. Maybe I need therapy. Maybe I am the problem.

As I pull into the main parking lot, I see an ambulance and a police car. I'm not alarmed, just curious if Simone is here. I walk toward the vehicles but they both pull out simultaneously as I approach.

I stand just outside the administration building door and Tory, the cafe owner, comes out and grabs my arm. She yanks me around the side of the tall shrubs that flank the doors. "There you are," she blurts out in one gasp. "Were you involved in this? I'm not surprised you're here. Another death! I'm afraid they'll close this place and I'll be out of work. Stay away, will you?" She fumes.

"Another death?" I ask. 'I don't know anything about it. Let go of me."

She drops my arm. "It's that English woman. The snoopy one, sort of like you."

"Sarah Jane!" I worry, mouthing her name. "What about her?"

"Rumor has it she fell in the park and, well, maybe, died. At least that's what that little boy was screaming as he raced into the building.

"Little boy? Rumor… so nothing definite?" I take a breath. "Wait, was he a red-headed boy with unruly hair?"

"Yep. He and his parents came in very upset. The boy was, well, rather excited by it, and the parents were almost hiding behind him, mortified. He said there was a woman laying dead in the woods below Inspiration Point and she didn't move when he poked her. And then the authorities showed up...'

"Simone?" I ask breathlessly.

"Is that her name?" Tory gasps. "Poor Simone."

"No, Simone is the detective – here investigating Derek's death. I know you've talked with her."

"Oh. Yeah. Simone – tall black woman – serious, demanding. Not sure I like her – "

"Yeah, well, she was doing a job. But anyway, the English woman was Sarah Jane – Sarah Jane Pratt. Are you saying she was found at the bottom of Inspiration Point?"

"That seems to be it."

I stare at her for a full minute. Then turn my back to her and slowly walk to the car. What should I do? Was it really Sarah Jane? Is she dead? And that sweet little red-headed boy, 'ginger' Sarah Jane called him. Did he find her? I need to place another call to Simone.

After I unlock the driver's side, I notice something under the windshield wiper. In annoyance, I grab it, tearing it as I pull it hard toward me. I look down and see the scrawled letters.

SARAH JANE PRATT – SPLATT!!!

My eyes stare unblinking at the words. I feel lightheaded, dizzy. As I stagger against my car, the paper falls from my hand and tears form in my eyes. I drop to the ground and put my head in my hands. Poor Sarah Jane. What has happened to her? Who would write such a cruel note?

A bark of laughter from far off in the lot brings me to. When I look up, I see the torn paper skipping across the pavement. Rising quickly to my feet, I race after it. When I'm clutching it in my hand, I rip open the car door, start the engine and roar off home. To my porch. To summon Simone. As I stop at the traffic light on Gibsonia Road, I take a deep breath and wipe tears from my eyes. What was Sarah Jane saying? She needed to meditate?

Robert's Story VII

I need the van to pick up supplies ordered by Bobby and Sebastian. When I go behind the restaurant, it's not there. I remember I haven't picked up the key from the hook inside so I go in to check for it. Sure enough, it's missing.

No one else is here, so I leave Bobby a message telling him the van is out so these last supplies won't be here when he gets in this afternoon. Maybe he has the van, I think. Or Jake might have made a run for him. If so, someone will show up with those supplies. I busy myself arranging shelves so I can load more after the new stuff arrives. Just then Terence walks in. He is singing "Highway to the Danger Zone" and seems loose and happy.

"Hey, good to see you," I call. Then I notice he is hanging up the van key. "So you brought the van back. Great. I've got an errand. Where have you been?"

"Ah, just picking something up."

"What? Is it still in the van?"

"Uh, no. Dropped it off."

I give him a sly smile. "Personal errand?"

"What's with the third degree? The van's all yours." He turns his back on me and acts like he's checking the stove. He never uses the stove.

"Ok," I say. "See 'ya." Terence sometimes seems so simple and other times is an enigma. Maybe we should use him more in the restaurant, get him more invested. I think about this as I pull the van out onto High Street.

~32~

My English friend

Once I am firmly ensconced on my porch with a strong cup of Earl Grey tea, I again put in a call to Simone. No answer. Into the tea I have added a bit of milk. Like my English friend. In honor of (not in memory of – I'm not believing that) Sarah Jane. I have two cups, vacuum my living room, make dinner, and finally I see Simone pull up. I know she finds Sarah Jane as charming as I do. I'm almost afraid to hear what she has to say but the only way to alleviate my fear is to hear from her. I go to the front door to wave her in but she troops in the side door, like family. As she is, I think.

"I heard something really bad at the park," I say. "Really bad. Another incident."

She looks at me with sad eyes. I fear the worst is true.

"Oh Kate," she begins.

"Then Sarah Jane is hurt?"

"Yes, she's in the hospital. Her husband is with her. She's unconscious with broken bones."

"I need to go see her. She's a good friend. So full of life and adventure."

"No, you can't talk to her right now."

"I could support her husband. I could help out somehow. I could… Who would want to hurt her?"

"Who? It looks like an accident. I'm assuming she lost her footing and fell. Maybe she heard something and went to the edge of the bluff for a better look. I'm speculating, of course."

"The poor vicar. Sarah Jane told me she was going to eat some lunch and meditate. She wasn't happy about being away from home so long. I hope she didn't lay there long. And I hear it was my little friend, the hiking boy who found her."

"Well that's a tragedy too. A small boy coming upon an injured, unconscious person. At least his parents were a few feet behind him."

"I bet they were," I think. And then I raise a finger to Simone and say, "Wait here."

I go to the garage and, with a tissue wrapped around my hand, grab the torn paper from the front seat of the car.

"Look what I found on my windshield just after the ambulance left."

Simone leans toward to the paper and looks it over. "How much have you handled this?" she asks.

"Well, I pulled it from underneath the wiper, read it, dropped it, then later grabbed it as it blew across the lot. Then I laid it on the seat beside me. After I got home I realized it was evidence so I left it in the car and just now picked it up with my hand in this tissue."

Simone takes out a glove and a bag and collects the paper.

"We'll look for prints."

"Do you have Margot's on file?" I ask. "Sarah Jane had overheard some interesting comments when she was inside the

Administration building. Margot came out of the offices and realized that Sarah Jane may have heard some private words. She darted back into the offices just before Sarah Jane left for her," I pause to collect myself, "her hike." I tear up. Simone hugs me once more time and sits me down and hands me my tea.

Simone raises her eyes to think. "So, let me see if I have this straight. This morning or about lunch time, Sarah Jane was in the administration building and overhead Margot saying some..."

"To be clear, according to Sarah Jane it was Margot and Larry she heard. Or maybe Larry didn't say anything but she was talking to him. Margot told Larry to behave himself and that she can't keep covering for him. Yeah, that's the phrase."

Simone says nothing for a long minute. "Let me think." She looks at the plastic bag in her hand. "I don't have Larry's or Margot's fingerprints as there were no prints at the scene of the body. So no prints were taken."

"But now maybe you should."

"I'll get someone on it. When Sarah Jane is coherent, I hope we'll learn more." She looks at the evidence bag in her hand. "But I don't like this note. Not one bit."

"I thought there was something odd..."

"Don't jump ahead. It's most likely harmless. Two employees who don't like each other or maybe vie for the attention of John or, well, I don't know. Give me time to check this out. Also, after you arrived at the building this morning when the note was placed on your car, how long were you there? Was Margot around? Or Larry for that matter?"

"I pulled in and saw the emergency vehicles, got out of my

car and tried to approach them, thinking you were in the police car, but they pulled out. Then I walked to the outside of the front door. And, at this point, Tory came out and grabbed my arm and told me what was going on."

"So, you exited your car. You were not looking at the building at that time, correct?"

"Yes."

"And how long were you engaged in trying to approach the emergency vehicles?"

"Not long. Like less than thirty seconds."

"Then, you headed to the building and would have been visible through the glass doors, right?"

"Yep. I was standing about to open a door when Tory came dashing out."

"So you stood there with Tory and talked for about how long?"

"Oh, about a minute or two. I was in a bit of shock at her news that the emergency involved Sarah Jane."

"But, assuming Margot was in the building, she couldn't have exited with you standing there or you would have seen her. Right?"

I think. "Well actually, Tory grabbed my arm and pulled me around the bushes at the corner of the building. And I had my back to the door area. So, I'm not exactly sure what went on behind me. And I'm not sure why Tory decided to pull me around the bushes."

"And by the time you get to your car there is a paper on the windshield. Did someone in the building have time to write a note and place it under your wiper?"

"Sure. I guess."

"So someone had time to get paper, write this out and sneak it to your car. That's pretty fast work."

"I think it was Margot. Who has more paper at the ready than Margot?"

Simone ponders. She takes her hands and rubs her face. Then she looks at the note contained the plastic bag.

"I believe I have seen a Sharpie on that counter of hers."

~33~

A large wrench

S imone has gone off to do her official work. I grab my book and begin to read on the porch. The wind is up and I wrap in a warm throw. After a couple of pages I stop to think.

John, Margot, Larry. None of them seem to get along. They argue like family. Sarah Jane's reporting from 'the stall' indicates they bicker with each other. Bickering at work? That's a bad office.

I think about all the suspects on the crime board. I need to refocus my efforts. Dale thinks it's Michael Sespin. Dale should have some insight. I stare across the street and think. Suddenly the park workers fade and all I can see is Michael spitting on the ground where Derek was found. I open my eyes wide. "You fool, you have been distracted by those three park stooges."

I decide to walk down to the restaurant where Robert and company are working. I need to tell him about Sarah Jane. I'm able to get inside and see Sebastian behind the bar mixing alcohols together. "Back at it." I comment.

"Yep. Trying out more cocktails. I'm getting quite the repertoire, and this one is good. Let me make you one."

"I'll pay for it."

"No. There is no price for it yet. It's a test. Tell me what you think."

While he starts pouring and then shaking, I peer into the kitchen. It looks clean and ready to go but I know there is still much to do before opening. I see movement under the sink and there is Robert, laying on his back with a large wrench in his hands. Just then Sebastian walks in, handing me a stemmed crystal glass filled with a lovely light amber liquid. Taking a sip, I turn to the sink in time to see Robert emerge. He looks wet.

"You look a bit wet, dear," I call. "Any success?"

"Yup. I am awesome." He laughs. "Hey, what are you drinking?"

"A late afternoon cocktail by one of Pittsburgh's premier mixologists. And it is delicious."

"Don't have Sebastian make you a drink, Mom. He's really busy growing the specialty cocktail list."

"He handed it to me and asked me to try it. What could I do? Try a sip."

Robert stands up and takes the goblet from my hand. "Excellent, Seb," he says. "Put it on the list."

"What should I call it?"

"How about the Amber Wrench?"

"Well, I'll think about it," he retorts as we leave the kitchen.

"Ugh," I say. "Who wants to suck on a wrench?"

Robert shrugs. I grab his arm and look up at him.

"Robert," I begin. "I came here for a sad purpose. Something bad has happened."

He sighs heavily. "Let me have it. What?"

"Sarah Jane."

"Oh, our English rose. Something bad happened to her?"

"Yes, she had a fall in Rob Ryan Park and, well, she's was hurt."

"Injured? She fell?"

"When I went to the park this morning there was an ambulance in the lot and then Tory, you know Tory?"

"Nope. Is that the woman who works in the office you seem to have run-ins with"?

"No, that's Margot. Tory runs the Cafe."

"So what about Tory?"

"She told me that the ambulance was there for my friend the English woman who had fallen in the park."

"So maybe she is OK. Maybe Sarah Jane is just hurt a bit."

"No, Simone came by earlier and told me that Sarah Jane was injured badly. Knock on the head. Broken leg." I stare at Robert. "I can't bear it."

Robert puts his arms around me and hugs me. "Aw, Mom. What a thing to happen when she's so far from home. Sarah Jane. This is so sad."

I pull away a bit. "She fell off Inspiration Point."

Robert thinks. "I know that spot. It's not that high. It's not on a cliff or anything. No rocks around. I don't understand how that could have happened." He shakes his head.

"What's more, I got a note on my windshield."

"What kind of note?"

"It said 'Sarah Jane Pratt, Splat.'"

"What! Did you tell Simone? That's sinister."

"Yeah. It was put there while I was parked at the park."

Robert look down, rubbing his forehead. "So, you're not

going back there, right? Please. Promise me. If you get the urge to go there just… just stop by here and Sebastian will mix you a calming concoction. But I beg you to stay away from that place."

I look at Robert and realize I owe it to my son to tell him everything I know, everything that happened. I begin with Dale's visit to the house, which stuns him. Then add that Sarah Jane and I had been seen outside of his house. And that he had told Sarah Jane not to hang around with me. It was hard to tell him all this. He is pacing in frustration and, frankly, angry that I would put myself at risk. When I finish my confession, he is very quiet. After a minute or two he insists he is going to tell Simone to put an order out that I am not allowed in the park. He complains that he is frazzled by the work and I am making his life harder. He repeatedly rubs his head and paces around dining room.

I promise him that I will be careful but I stop short of saying I won't go to the park. I can't let Sarah Jane's 'accident' go unaddressed. Splat! indeed. You just don't read a note like that and not do anything. I am beginning to regret my honesty to Robert.

He stops pacing and points at me. "Someone once warned you things happen in threes. Listen to her!"

Robert's Story VIII

I find myself sitting at the bar staring at the bottles Sebastian has carefully arranged on the lighted shelves that rise up on the wall behind. They look enticing, lovely even. If I were a drinker I would open one up and start chugging. My mother is driving me crazy. And now I am spent and slumped on this bar stool. I keep capping and uncapping a cocktail shaker, trying to figure out how to stop my mind from reeling. And then, on cue, Terence walks in wearing bright red floppy shoes.

"Have a night job in the circus?" I ask, a small smile beginning to turn up the edges of my mouth.

"Huh, what?" he stammers. I point to his feet.

"You've seen these. I had them on that day I, er, kind of broke some dishes."

"Were they red like that?"

"Yes. I kind of, well, like red."

"Well thanks. You've improved my mood."

"What's wrong, Robert?"

"Oh, my mother and her sleuthing and now a friend of hers has been injured at the park and a threatening note was put on my mother's windshield, and... Oh, forget it. I'll deal with it."

"Wow. Sounds bad. You know, Robert, I heard Bobby talking about getting a dessert supplier... you know someone who would bake and deliver daily desserts here to the restaurant.

What about your mother? She's a great baker. And it would give her something else to think about."

I look at Terence in surprise. First, because he is being really thoughtful and second, because I don't understand why he thinks my mother is a great baker.

"She's not a great baker," I finally say. "Not sure where you got that idea."

"Well, um..." Terence scratches his head. "I thought I heard someone say that."

"I doubt it."

Terence looks nervous. "Ok, well I'm off. Just brought the van back. Good night!"

"See ya. I'm heading out too."

I lock up and walk slowly back to my place. I think a lot about Terence. He's such a nice guy but so ... I can't come up with the right word. He is so Terence, I decide. I think about what he said about my mother being a good baker. Did someone really say that? Does my mother think she's a baker? I put in a call to Bobby.

"Hey man, I have a question."

Bobby replies. "Shoot."

"Did you say we need a dessert supplier and my mother is a possibility?"

"Yes and no. Need desserts... don't know anything about your mother. Is she a baker?"

"No, just something Terence said."

"Oh, well speaking of mothers. I'm with mine now and she has this clay fire pot that is cooking out on her patio. I am loving this. Just kicking back and enjoying the embers and the heat." He sighs.

"Did you buy it for her?"

"No, not sure where she got it but it is a great addition to the cement slab behind her house."

I think about Terence and those ridiculous shoes. I think about why he thinks my mother can bake. I think about how he had the van out tonight. I call Mom.

"Hey, can you look out back and see if the chiminea is still there?"

"Huh, why wouldn't it be?"

"Just look. I'm doing a bit of sleuthing on my own."

"Hang on." I hear her open the slider to the patio.

"Oh no, it's gone. How did you know? Did you see little Freddie from next door messing about here tonight?"

"No, I don't suspect Freddie. I'll be in touch." I hang up.

-34-

Pain meds

I don't care what they said about going to see Sarah Jane in the hospital. I stop by the restaurant to check in with Robert on my way. What about that chiminea? But he's not at the bistro. But before I take off, I have a nice talk with Jake, the sous chef. I tell him about the Victoria sponge walking off the porch. Jake laughs at the image of a cake walking away by itself and asks, "Didn't the dish run away with the spoon?" After I chuckle with him, I bring down our moods to get serious and tell him about Sarah Jane's accident. He seems sincerely concerned, wishing her well enough to come to the opening of the bistro. I smile at him, pat him on the hand, and head to my car.

I pull into the lot at Passavant Hospital. When I find her room in the labyrinth of hallways, there she is, looking miserable, her leg hanging from a contraption.

"I was so worried about you," I exclaim, grabbing her hand. "What happened?"

"I'm exhausted. I just told everything I know to Simone. But I think, and I wonder if I am remembering this right, I think I saw a rope hanging from a tree over the drop off at Inspiration Point. And it had a noose at the end."

"What!? Oh my God. Sarah Jane."

"I don't know. My head is still a bit fuzzy and they gave me pain meds but I'm sure I remember this."

"And you told Simone?"

"Yes, I did. Just now. The noose. I remember I tried to grab at it. It seemed a bad thing to have hanging there and when I reached out my hand..."

"What?" I am sitting so close to the edge of the vinyl hospital chair that I almost slip off.

"I guess I lost my footing. It's just that I only leaned a bit and then I was falling, head over heels."

"You were pushed," I conclude.

"I don't remember that. I just launched into the air and then all is, well, black."

"So there was a rope, maybe a noose, hanging from a tree off the trail?"

"I think so, maybe. But the police didn't find it there so I must have imagined it."

"Why would you imagine a noose?"

"I don't think I did, but, Simone looked at me like I was crazy."

She has a tear running down her cheek and I remember that she is hurt and far from home and probably scared. "It'll be OK," I say. "Don't worry about it. That's Simone's job."

I wonder if Simone has told her about the note? I hope not.

"How long do you have to have your foot up there?" I change the subject, pointing to her dangling leg.

"I should be out of this soon. Then on crutches. But now, just to make things harder, John is called back home. I'm not sure I can do this on a plane. He has pleaded to stay but something has come up. It's so frustrating. When we wanted to leave they insisted he stay longer and now that we have this complication," she points to her leg, "they insist he fly home."

"You'll stay with me until you can fly comfortably," I conclude.

"No, I cannot be a burden." Sarah Jane now has three tears running down her face.

"I would love it," I gush. "I would adore it. You can be here for the restaurant opening. I know you'll miss John, but maybe he can come back in a couple weeks or, well, whatever his and your time frame demand, and then..."

Sarah Jane smiles. "You are too sweet and there is no one I would be more comfortable staying with than you, but, this is something I have to think on."

"Talk to your doctors and your husband and just know it's on the table," I say.

She smiles and nods and then gives a big yawn.

"I'm out of here. Rest up. You have my number. Call if you need anything – anything," I reiterate.

Robert's Story IX

I walk out the back door for air. The inside air is getting rarified and I get why. We're getting closer to opening and emotions are rising. Jake is outside the backdoor. Smoking a joint, as always. It's how he cooks best he says, and there is no doubt he's a great sous chef and melds with Bobby quite well.

"How's it going, man?" I ask, as I sit next to him on a crate.

"How are things in there?" he replies, hooking his thumb and pointing to the door.

"I think very well." I smile, knowing that Bobby and Sebastian will bring it home. God knows I'll bust my ass to make sure they have all they need.

"Cool. Very cool. When I first talked to Bobby about working here, he explained the dynamics and I wasn't sure about you. But now I get it. You're good at defusing their craziness and that will keep the place sane. Neither of those two loonies can defuse a situation. Maybe Sebastian at the bar – he's good with a drunk. But staff and dining patrons, you have it there man."

"Why thank you."

"Where'd you learn to be so placating and mellow?"

"Uh, I don't know. It's my nature."

"Your mom was just here. You missed her by half an hour."

"Really? Big surprise. Try to keep her out. She lives a few blocks away."

"No complaint. She's a nice person… and funny. She had me laughing. I think maybe you get some of your talents from her."

"I don't want her talents. They seem to mainly consist of coming upon crimes and bodies."

"What do you mean?" Jake turns to me. "Seriously man, What-Do-You-Mean?"

"Did you hear about the dead man in Rob Ryan Park – it's only about twenty minutes from here? Well, my mom is the one who found the body."

"How awful! How… what.. did she see it laying somewhere? Trip over it?"

"That would be too ordinary for my mother. She has her style to maintain. No, she grabbed the corpse's hand as she was falling into the creek."

"Huh? Where was the corpse?"

"Buried in the trail, except for its hand protruding out the side of the wall of the ravine."

"Whoa." He shakes his head. "Not sure I've ever been to that park."

"Well, I'm thinking about going over there because I bet my mother is heading there. She has this idea that the murderer is lurking in the park. Not sure what she is thinking exactly, maybe the murderer is looking for another victim or reliving the crime. I tell her to stay away but she keeps going back."

"Really!!!?? So she is trying to solve the crime?"

"Oh, yeah. You know Simone? Tall black woman who has been in here a couple of times?"

"Yes, very impressive she is. She's a detective."

"Yes, and my mom and her are friends due to another crime my mother was privy to."

Jake stands abruptly. "So maybe that's why she comes here. Trying to solve the crime. Does this place have anything to do with the investigation?" His eyes are wide.

"Nothing, I think. But, well, never mind. Let's just say my mother likes a free drink which Sebastian has been handing out lately."

"Oh. Agree with you. Let Simone solve the crime. Your mom should stay home and avoid that park."

"But she doesn't. Like I said, she's over there listening around corners, walking trails..."

"Let's go do that. It sounds like fun. Let's go walk trails, listen to conversations, scope out the crime scene. Do you know where she found the body?"

"I do."

"Let's go. Get your stuff. This'll be a trip."

I look at Jake like he's crazy, which he is, and then I think maybe he could put a fresh perspective on the scene and we could do a bit of fact-finding at the park together.

I nod. "We could use a little recreation."

~35~

Basketball shoes

I come home to grab a coat and as I pull into the driveway, Lois from across the street waves at me.

"Did I see Simone over there?"

"Oh, yeah. You know she's a friend."

"Did she say anything about robberies in the neighborhood? Daryl's favorite shoes are missing."

I think about that. Most likely they are misplaced, although I have seen Daryl's shoes when he is outside. Big feet he has. And likes bright basketball shoes. They might be hard to misplace. Who would take old stinky shoes? But then I think about the chiminea and the Victoria sponge. Is there a crime wave here? I look over to Lois.

"I haven't heard of robberies," I lie. "Well, except Junie seems to have a lost a potted plant. And, FYI, Simone was just here socializing."

"OK, well let me know. I don't trust this place ever since, you know." She points a finger at the garden next door to her house. There was a body there a couple of years ago and Lois is still nervous, even though Simone figured out what happened.

"Sure," I say. "Hope those shoes turn up." I trip into the

house, thinking about dinner and wondering if I should mention the missing items to Simone. I know she doesn't work in the robbery division but they could be related to the murder, maybe. I mean, it's my chiminea that's missing, Junie knew Derek, Sarah Jane was at the park a lot. And we all have experienced a loss. Might be worth mentioning.

As I start dinner I can see Kay from next door working the fallen leaves in her yard. I head over. "Hi neighbor," I greet her. "I just talked to Lois and she said Darryl's shoes are missing."

"Big deal. Brad says his golf clubs walked off. I think they are in someone else's trunk by mistake or maybe at a course, but he insisted he propped them outside of the garage after he got back from a round."

"Our chiminea is gone. And, even weirder, a friend made a special cake for us for dessert and it was on the porch waiting for us to cut it and it disappeared."

"Hmm. Crime returns to the neighborhood. Any idea who is responsible?"

"Robert acted like he had an idea about the chiminea. I'll check with him and get back to you. Sorry about the clubs. Those are expensive."

"Maybe you should tell our ace detective Simone."

"I'm on it."

Robert's Story X

*J*ake and I pull into the Visitors area. We walk into the building. It's late, after four, and there aren't a lot of people around. The woman is not behind the counter that dominates the area in front of the offices. The doors are closed. It seems quitting time has passed.

Jake grabs a map from the stand and spreads it open. "Come here, Rob. Where was this body found?"

I point to the Ravine trail.

"Get us there," he directs. "Lead us on over."

And so I do. We soon find ourselves sitting on the edge of the Ravine Trail looking into the creek below. Jake hands me a lit joint and I suck in the smoke. Soon we are blindly staring into the water. The woods are quiet with just the low sound of running water.

And then I spy a man way down in the creek, carefully stepping along the edge of the water, avoiding rapids as best he can, occasionally jumping onto a rock exposed in the water.

"Do you see him?" I ask Jake, grabbing his arm and pointing toward the lone figure below.

"Sure do."

We don't say anything for a while. Just watch. The man seems pretty good at this. It looks dangerous to me but he seems steady.

"That looks crazy," Jake finally says. At this the man looks up and sees us. Jake waves. The man doesn't acknowledge his greeting and puts his head down, continuing on until he is out of site. "Looked like a soldier didn't he," Jake says. "All camoed up. Maybe he's on a pretend mission. You know, stalking the enemy on the Yang Dang River or something."

"Yang Dang River?" I ask.

"I made that up." Jake laughs. "You're easy."

I pick a yellow flower that is growing at the edge of the bank and twirl it in my hands. Jake continues to stare down into the ravine. After a few minutes he looks at me and says, "Your mom fell down this embankment? Scary."

"Frankly, the dead man's hand helped break her fall. In death he may have saved a life. How do you like that?" We start to giggle.

"Remind me, who was the guy who died? You told me but I don't remember."

"Some guy who gave a lot of money to the park and was trying to buy land to increase its size. A nature lover."

"Why would someone kill him? I mean, if he was generous then....oh wait. Had a lot of money and someone wanted to get their hands on it. Old story."

"As I said before, Simone is figuring that out... with interference from the local amateur detective."

"Your mom is the amateur?" Jakes grins.

"Yeah. And she is obsessed with helping her figure it all out."

I shrug and we continue watching the creek. The quiet is almost deafening. Jake leans back. And then, without warning, a walnut flies by his head and bounces on the ground. I bend over in laughter as he turns quickly, looking for a squirrel in the tree above.

"Thanks squirrel," I say. "He needed a wake up call."

And then I find a couple of walnuts pelting the ground around me.

"These things would hurt if they made a direct hit."

We both look up, but in the dense foliage, but we can't see anything.

"Is that a squirrel?" Jake questions.

"Maybe a big mean one."

Then, just as we are laughing at ourselves, a barrage of at least five walnuts comes down near our heads. We jump to our feet and stand in the middle of the trail, whirling to see where they came from.

Jake points. "Look, look at that."

"I don't see anything.'

"It was a boot landing on the ground behind the ground cover. I swear there was a camo pant leg attached."

"Camo pant leg, you said? Like the guy walking the creek?"

"Yeah. How did he sneak up here without us hearing him?"

"And he climbed a tree and threw stuff at us? What's that about?"

"Creek man was attacking us?"

We crash into the woods but don't see him. Everything quiets for a minute but then we hear a laugh. 'Goobers!" a voice yells from far away.

We sit back down. The adrenaline rush has died and we are mellow again. I toss one of the walnuts in the air and catch it in my palm. "I've never been attacked by walnuts," I comment.

"Walnuts? Those are walnuts?" Jake picks up one still in its green hull. "This is a walnut?"

"Yep, chef. This is where walnuts come from."

"Where is the walnut?"

"Duh, inside the casing."

Jake turns one over in his hand. "My training was lax. We didn't discuss how walnuts grow."

Again, he fondles the nut. "So inside this green thing is our friendly and tasty walnut. How do you get it out?"

"Brute force, I guess."

We both tap on a nut. "Why did he ping these at us? I mean he could have beaned us and that might have been bad. Especially with your fragile head."

"I know. In fact, when you think about it, it wasn't funny."

Jake stands. "Let's go. It's getting dark and weirdo is still out there. Goobers! Doesn't he know goobers are peanuts. He was throwing walnuts."

We dust off our pants and head out.

~36~

Three amigos

It's about two when I hear the wail of my doorbell. I'm watching the Steelers. When I throw open the door, it's Simone. With a pizza in her hand.

"Hungry?" she asks with a big grin on her face. "I am and I picked up a hot pizza. Get plates." She glances at the TV. "And you have the Steelers on. It's a regular party."

"They're behind," I say. "Sit down and I'll get the plates and napkins." I walk into the kitchen. "Do you want a fork?" I call back into the living room.

"No, no need."

We each grab a slice of pizza and I sit down on the couch. Simone sits in the leather chair. We both stare at the TV which is now showing a rowdy beer commercial.

"Did you want beer?" I ask her.

"No, water is good. But sit still, I can get myself some later."

The pizza is hot and very good. I like the green peppers. I start on piece two.

Simone looks over at me. "I visited the Three Amigos Venture Company."

"What's that?" I ask, thinking she is making a joke.

"It's the group that wants to buy the farm that Derek wanted and, as you know, suspects. Remember, one of them is Jim from the bistro."

"Oh I know him, but what I didn't know is that the group had such a catchy name. What were you doing there?"

"I had a few follow-up questions from a couple of days ago. And I think I may have hit upon something."

"Do tell," I say while chewing.

"So, as you know, this case is tough. Body found who knows how long after death. Rain- soaked ground, body and clothes wet and, thus, fingerprint-less. If you want to kill someone, burying them where they won't be found for a long time is a good cover. Anyway, I was told to wait with the assistant in the Amigos front office. She kept looking at me and then turning away and then fidgeting and looking at me again so I asked, 'What is it that you want to tell me?' I decoded her body language well because then she looked behind her at the closed door and turned to me and said, 'I am worried about something I heard.' So I said, 'You should never keep anything from the police in a murder investigation. It's possible if we found out you were holding back that you could be in trouble.' And she said, 'It's just that I heard them – the three amigos, talking about it a week ago. Almost laughing. They were discussing how the body was buried and how timely was the death, and well, they were being cruel.' Then she hesitated and added, 'Not only cruel, but congratulatory in a way.'"

Simone stops.

I say, "Whoa. Interesting,"

"Yep. So I ask her to come to the station and make a

statement and when she does, she hints that the Amigos are turning into enemies over this. They are pointing fingers at each other. So now, I am thinking I may be able to get them to sell each other out. This is a hopeful development for me. I'm going to call them all into the station and talk to them separately and hint at what the others might have said and, frankly, make them squirm. Awesome, isn't it?"

"I guess that's a police technique. Seems a long shot to me."

"You don't know how convincing I can be. And I can get a good cop-bad cop thing going. Frankly, I don't think they'll know what hit them."

"You really think they, or one of them, is responsible?"

"I'm starting to. And there is another reason. I heard from the farm owner that two weeks ago they had indicated to everyone involved that they were strongly leaning toward Derek. I think that panicked our Three Amigos."

"Whoa. They would be some upsetting news. A couple of weeks ago you say?"

Simone sighs. "This seems my best bet. Besides, my other leads are going nowhere. And other than Dale, who did have a lot to gain from Derek's death? No one else benefited as much. But after spending time with Dale, I'm not sure he has the gumption to pull off a murder. He seems to have a lot of humanity."

We finish our pizza and watch some more of the game. I say, "I think Robert might have an idea who took our Victoria sponge the other day."

Simone looks at me. "That's it, turn the subject to a missing cake. Oh, and did you see Sarah Jane? I had a nice talk with her."

"Yep." And I reiterate my conversation.

"Oh, I almost forgot. You know the rope burn on Derek's neck and the noose Sarah Jane claims she saw? Well, in my background check on one the Amigos, I discover he spent a bit of time out west competing in rodeo competitions back in the day. What do you think of that?"

"Weird, but OK. I guess people do that."

"Well, he did and I will be pointing that out to his two other Amigos at the interrogation. I almost can't wait."

"So you've ruled out Dale. You know he surprised me by stopping by my house one day. Margot gave him my address."

"Why didn't you tell me this? Why would he even know who you are?"

"Because I was at the memorial service and I, well, did what I always do and spilled the beans about finding the body. He was very nice about it. Seemed concerned that I had to go through such a grisly experience."

"What was his attitude when he was at your house – intimidating, or …?"

"At first I felt threatened, he was only on the porch, but then, honestly, he seemed nice and a bit confused and lost. I'm still not sure why he stopped by, but in the end it was fine."

"Let me mull this over. The thing about Dale is that he is a bit of a sad sack. God, I hope that's not an act that he's pulling off. He told me he and Derek got along fine before Derek made his money but that Derek got tight fisted after that. And, you told me you saw him and Chloe together?"

I nod.

"Well he said she has been a friend to him even though he knows she is angling for the promised donation to her school."

I think a minute and then ask, "What about Michael Sespin, Rhonda's brother? He was spouting venom when I saw him at the trail site."

"I question how he could he pull off the death and burial alone.""

"Maybe Chloe and Dale helped him."

"Far-fetched, I think."

"But why is Michael here now?"

"It's a good question. And records show he has been here for a bit. What seems to be the truth is that he was in touch with Dale and when Dale came to town to see Derek, Michael thought he would come too and try to join forces with him to carry out Rhonda's wishes with the school."

"So Dale and Michael are in touch? Why?"

"Don't know. But the Three Amigos are my focus now. Although I am going to have another talk with the humble Dale. And, I don't like Michael being here."

Simone stands and paces. "This bunch is driving me crazy – three amigos, one brother, not to mention one brother-in-law." She plops down in the chair, thinking.

"What about the fingerprints you were going to take from the Administration staff"?

Simone smiles. "Yes, your theory. My sergeant is getting those – should have them in fact. Thanks for bringing that up."

Simone looks to the television and then to the empty pizza box.

"This game seems to be in the bag and the pizza is gone. Gotta get back to it. See you soon."

And she is off.

-37-

Who are the others

After the game, I decide to have a good think about what Simone told me. I brew a cup of tea and sit down in front of my crime board. She is focusing on the Three Amigos but I think I gave her more to think about after I recounted Dale's visit. I'm still not sure of anything. There must be something to the Dale, Michael, Chloe relationships. Dale gets money. Chloe gets money. Michael gets revenge. I look at the property developers picture on the crime board. I should change that to the Three Amigos. I know Jim Tucci, but who are the others? I grab my computer and google.

On the Three Amigos website the three are in a jovial pose in western hats, chin straps dangling. One even has what looks like a false mustache. I note the other two names: James Berkey and Robin McNabb. I add their names to the crime board after copying and printing the image of the three from the website.

I slowly go from face to face on the board. There is Derek. It is sad to see him next to Rhonda. A couple who died too soon. Then Dale, Michael, Chloe. They look disjointed to me. Like three very different people. But apparently they have some knowledge of each other. And the Amigos. I go back to their website which is still up on my computer. Oh, they developed that cute mixed use area off Route 228. Small specialty shops, cute restaurants. I like that place. But that image of the three of them says 'banditos'.

I shake my head and pick up the latest mystery I am reading. I know this crime in a small English town will be solved. Of Derek's murder, I'm not so sure.

Robert's Story XI

$\mathcal{I}$ walk into the bistro the next morning, ready to organize plates. The new ones are in and I am trying to figure out the best spot to stock them so they are easily available to the chefs and cooks but also accessible to the dishwasher. I'm thinking we may need a bit of chrome shelving when Bobby comes out of the cooler, muttering.

"What's up?" I say, not sure I really want to know.

"Jake. Where the hell is he? We made a date to work on the steak options and he doesn't show."

"Dunno."

Sebastian strolls into the kitchen. He picks up a lime and rolls it around on the counter.

"You seen Jake?" Bobby asks him.

"Briefly. He was in early. I was surprised to see him that early actually. He was messing about in the storage area and then came bounding out front and said he was off to harvest walnuts. Was that a thing you guys are doing?"

"Walnuts?" both Bobby and I exclaim together.

"I think that's what he said."

"He's lost his mind," Bobby retorts. "I knew it was going to happen eventually but not this soon."

"Actually," I begin. "Actually, Jake and I were in the woods last night, hiking about, and we ran into some downed walnuts.

He was intrigued seeing them in their natural state. Perhaps he decided to fetch some this morning."

"What do you mean 'in their natural state'?"

"In their hulls. He didn't know walnuts started life like that."

"We get our walnuts in bags from the supplier. We don't harvest walnuts. Anyway, they wouldn't be the same as those we buy. Did you suggest this?"

"No. Just identified them as walnuts."

"The fool."

"I think he'll be back soon with a few walnuts and a hammer," I laugh.

"He better get here like yesterday. Time is wasting."

~38~

A cloud of smoke

I'm back on my old walk around the neighborhood, trying hard to avoid the park since the Splat note.

I do like looking at other people walking and going down High Street. I like to see what's happening there. So much is always going on in the neighborhood. People have painters, plumbers, landscapers, HVAC vans, and all sorts of services crawling on their properties. I see an HVAC worker walking to his truck with a long, thin pipe. I see painters on scaffolding on a roof on Sutton Street. Later on Puff, I saw hedges being trimmed so expertly that they were smooth as a countertop. Everyone is busy. On the second loop of my walk, I pass by the new Bistro on High and stop in to say hello. I can't resist. Sebastian is standing behind the bar and it looks as if he's counting. His finger is extended and jumping up and down. I try not to startle him as his back is turned to me, but he still jumps when I say hello.

"Oh, hi Kate. Not sure Robert is still here. How are you?"

"Just popping in to be friendly," I say. "Things are really looking ready." I look around at the bar and dining area. Things are lined up and in place.

"Just checking what I have and putting together some procedures to follow."

"Ah," I say.

"I'm hiring another part time bartender. Someone coming in today. Looks good on paper but no one knows her. Most of the other people we've hired on have some connection to someone we know, but this woman is a stranger. I hope I like her. I don't like hiring."

"I thought Robert was doing interviewing."

"Yeah, he'll be here. But I need to have final say."

"Makes sense to me," I think.

Just then Robert walks in, carrying what look like heavy boxes. Sebastian steps forward to help. Robert looks at me and says, "Passing by, Mom?" He sounds exasperated. Could it be me he is exasperated with?

"As a matter of fact I was. Everyone is so busy here, and in the neighborhood too," I say. And I spend my time reading on my porch. The advantage of age." I smile. They pretty much ignore me.

"Good news, though. I'm walking in the neighborhood again. Avoiding the park. Man, I miss it."

"Excellent news!" Robert exclaims a bit too loudly. "I'm glad you have washed your hands of that place."

I start. "I haven't exactly washed…."

I'm interrupted by Bobby rushing in from the kitchen.

"Is Jake back?" he blurts out, looking sharply around the restaurant. "I heard the door and then someone said 'Excellent' so I assumed..."

Sebastian slowly shakes his head.

"Still no answer to his cell?" Bobby demands.

"Is he missing?" I venture.

"No, just his usual inconsiderate self," Bobby blurts out. "Someone may have to check out that park he was going to and see if he is sitting under a tree in a cloud of smoke hammering at walnuts." He suddenly smiles. "I'd pay for that pic."

"What park?" I demand, looking at Robert.

"The park, Mom."

"Jake is there and doing something with walnuts? And you can't locate him? With the recent history of that park, people need to be careful there." I give Robert a pleading look.

"Jake's fine. He's just unreliable and Bobby wants him here to do something and..."

"Want him here?" Bobby roars. "Expected him here first thing this morning. No sign of him. Not answering his phone."

"Why wouldn't he answer his phone?" I ask. "Aren't you worried? We could call Simone."

"Ok, calm down everyone. Jake just got sidetracked on this walnut thing and his phone is rarely charged."

"Walnut thing?" I inquire.

Sebastian jumps in. "Yep, he and Robert went to the park you know, where you found the body."

He looks at me knowingly. My mouth drops down in astonishment.

"And then these walnuts fell out of the tree and..."

"Correction, were tossed down at us," Robert interjects.

"Ok, were aimed at our two heroes and, voila, Jake discovers a native black walnut there. We use lovely English walnuts which are processed professionally and ready to use."

"Well, anyway," Sebastian continues, clearly enjoying telling the tale of Jake and the Walnuts, "Jake was fascinated and returned today, or so he said, to try his hand and bringing back walnuts. And he is either still there, harvesting away, or he has moved on to other places, one of which is not the kitchen of this establishment." He smiles and takes a small bow.

"Who or what was tossing walnuts?" I query, trying to get to what I think is the most interesting tidbit of this performance.

"A guy all done up in camo!" Sebastian extorts gleefully.

I freeze. Then turn to Robert.

"The camo guy?"

"He was walking the creek and somehow maneuvered behind us and the walnuts began falling and then, we saw a guy drop from the tree after, and Jake said his pant leg was camo. That's all. Just a joker."

"I know that joker. He pulled me out of the water. He was hiding off trail and made me get lost for a while. He has a beard, right?"

"Couldn't tell about a beard from up on the edge of the ravine."

"He called them goobers," Sebastian guffawed."

"I'm not really worried about some guy in a tree, but I am wondering if Jake got lost? He doesn't know his way around the woods." Robert finally seems to realize that maybe action needs to be taken. "I'm going to run over there and look around."

"Hang on, we have an interview in half an hour," Sebastian reminds Robert.

"OK, after that."

"Don't worry. I'll go." I chime in.

"No, Mom. Please don't. Let me call Jake again. He's probably back home having forgotten his appointment this morning and worn out from hiking and chasing walnuts." Robert picks up his phone. We all watch as he taps it and then puts it to his ear. Then he drops it to the side. "Nothing." he says.

"I can be there in twenty minutes or so," I insist.

"No, I'll go over in about an hour. He's fine."

"I can also call Simone."

"What does Simone have to do with this? Jake's only been missing for, I don't know, six hours. And his phone's dead. So, come on."

I turn to leave the bistro and as I do, Robert comes up behind me and pleads, "I'll go when I can and I'll call you when everything is fine."

Facing the group again, I point my finger. "We have a dead body buried under a trail. We have a note from someone at that place which points to Sarah Jane being pushed. We have someone traipsing around dressed like a soldier and messing about with people. There is something going on in that park and if you all think Jake is just merrily hiking along, I disagree. I'm going over there. Robert, you can follow in your own time. But I'm going now. You can ignore me or not. Everyone thinks I'm crazy anyway."

I look at each in turn. "You are bunch of goobers to laugh this off." And with that I spin and make a dramatic exit.

-39-

Menacing stare

When I arrive at the park I leap out of my car by the Administration Building. I'm not sure where to go first but wherever I do go, I have to get there fast. As my foot steps up on the sidewalk, I almost run into Simone. She stops, smiles, and gives me a big hug.

"You're something, you know?" she says, holding me in front of her by my shoulders.

"What?" I'm so confused by this that it takes me a minute to remember that I have to tell her about Jake and the camo guy and the walnuts and... But before I can say anything, she begins walking away at a strident pace. Then she stops and stares and I see what she is looking at. It's the khaki clad maintenance guy across the lot sitting on a mower glaring at us. Then I see his beard. I screw up my eyes. He looks like the guy who rescued me.

"Simone," I say, tagging her arm before she is out of reach, "who is that?"

"Larry Cloud. At least that's his name now." She give me a big grin. "Gotta go."

"Wait." I pull on her again. "But he has a beard. I thought

Larry didn't have a beard. And I swear he's the guy in the camo who pulled me from the creek."

Simone stares at Larry and then at me. "That's the guy? But that's the worker formally known as Larry."

I am so perplexed at what she is saying that I can't speak.

Simone goes on. "And what beard? That's not a beard."

"You don't see that beard hanging down off his chin?" I point. At this Larry, or whoever he is, starts up his mower and heads away from us. He looks back over his shoulder in a menacing stare.

"That's a bandana he hangs over his nose because he has allergies. I had to insist that he remove it when I interviewed him. He was reluctant, but admittedly he did begin to sneeze. But a beard?" She tilts her head to think. "OK, maybe I can see it. It's beige like his hair. But no time now. I have to go. Hey Larry!" The last two words she yells loudly.

But Larry has disappeared. Simone runs into the Administration building. I decide to head to my vantage point on Bunny Hill.

~40~

Play army

At the top of the hill I look over the park. Much of it is forest but there are open areas. I am trying to run into Jake which is admittedly like finding a needle in a haystack. But what other choice do I have? If only he'd pick up his phone. I can see a lot of cars entering into the upper ball field area, the ones on the other side of the park not near the Administration building. I can't imagine Jake would be interested in Little League. I wonder what Simone is up to. Why did she seem so pleased with me?

It seems eerily quiet on the hill today. No breeze. I sit down. My impetuous trip to the park is getting me nowhere. I should have queried Robert more to see if he could tell me where Jake might go. Where were those walnuts? I didn't think to ask. Some detective I am.

I scan the landscape below. And there, puttering into the open field of Bird Meadow, is Larry, swinging a rope. What is he doing? I squint. He has lassoed a large tree limb and, with his cart, he is dragging it to the side of the meadow. I stand for a better view. It's an amusement – the rope and the cart and the branch. Maybe he's not the threatening guy I thought he was.

Maybe he is boyish and playful. Perhaps I'm assigning him nefarious traits when he is an uncomplicated man.

I lay back and watch the clouds overhead. My mind wanders to Jake. Is he here in the park still looking for walnuts? Did I see any paths with walnuts laying about? I try to remember. I think of the Trillium Trail and the Ravine Trail. And what is the name of that trail that goes by Inspiration Point? I sit up abruptly. Oh, the noose Sarah Jane insists she saw there and the one Junie and I saw here. I glance around noting it is gone. And the rope burns Simone said were around Derek's neck. A chill washes over me. I stand and look down toward Larry in the meadow, but he is gone.

Robert's Story XIV

"**S**ebastian, Bobby – I have to go to the park. Sorry but you'll have to reschedule that interview. I'm going to chase down my mom before she gets herself in trouble." I grimace. "Maybe I'll find Jake."

I head to the door.

"Hold on," yells Sebastian. "I need you at this interview. It's late to cancel it. Just stay here for a bit. You know you can call your mother, right? Why don't you try her right now?"

I make the call but she doesn't answer. "Not picking up. Not sure why."

"Has she even made it to the park yet? Give it a bit. Maybe she doesn't use the phone in the car. Safety and all that."

"I don't know, Sebastian. But if something happens and I didn't try, well, how do I explain that?"

Sebastian considers. He nods. "Okay. Go Robert. But don't blame me if we hire a bad bartender."

I run for the door but look back. "Act like it's just a first interview and tell her we'll call her back if we like her."

The door slams behind me.

-41-

A grinding noise

I search below for Larry on his little vehicle. He seems to have melted away. I look right and left. Suddenly I feel very alone up here. I take a deep breath, but mid-exhale I hear a grinding noise – a mechanical motor. And around the far side of Bunny Hill comes Larry on his little vehicle, moving fast. I see his 'beard'. It really does look like a beard. He's looking at me intently. He's in his park clothes, the khaki's, but I think about the guy in the camo and I know now that was Larry too. He likes to play army in his off time, I think. I hear a phone ring and Larry stops, pulls a phone out of his pocket, looks at it, and tosses it into a copse of trees. I give him a confused look, but then remember the other abandoned phones. I'm even more curious about him now that I have put together the phone and the camo and the beard.

"You're Larry, aren't you?" I call loudly. "And you some-times wear camouflage. And you're the one who pulled me out of the creek." It all seems clear now. I just needed the 'beard' to paste it together. "You're two people," I say, with a laugh. The look on his face changes from an intense scowl to a vile expression. I back away a couple of steps. My phone rings and I see it's Robert calling. I glance up and Larry has moved closer to me. Nervously, I pocket my phone and then, on impulse, turn and run down the hill. He follows me on his scooter.

Robert's Story XIII

I arrive at the park and leave my car in the lot. I search for Mom's car, and there it is, parked a few rows in front of me. I run into the building but she's not in the entranceway or the little cafe. I dart to the exit and almost bowl over the woman who is normally at the front desk. "Get out of my way!" she screams. Her arms are full of papers. As I try to apologize, a man in a suit calls from the office door. "What did I say? Where are you going?" But the woman flees through the door and disappears. I look to the man. He straightens his tie, smiles at me, and asks, "Can we help you?" Without responding, I head out the door. My attention is captured immediately by squealing tires as a car barrels out of the lot. Where's Mom? This place is setting me on edge. I think of calling her again but she didn't answer the last time. No one picks up a phone. Not Jake, not Mom. Simone! Maybe I can get hold of her and then at least I can tell her to get over here. I punch in her number. The phone picks up and a man's voice says, "Yeah?"

~42~

Circling through
the meadow

Larry's cart is faster than I thought it would be. As I continue to run, I turn to check on his progress. He's keeping up, maybe gaining. I see the rope in his hand. It is attached to the back of the cart. I turn back and, when I get off the hill, I dash into Bird Meadow. Larry's vehicle bumps into the meadow as he attempts to follow me across the mown path. I dash sideways and drop into high grass. I hear the cart motor slow. I don't think he knows where I am. I catch my breath. And then he starts circling through the meadow. He's dropped the blade and is mowing round swaths in the grass. I lay quietly, hoping to stay concealed, but it's no use. His circular path will eventually find me. I wait until his back is turned then jump up and race onto the Trillium Trail. The trees should cover me, I think. But there is the noise again! He breaks onto the trail and, although there are roots and uneven ground, he seems to gain speed. He's close enough for me to hear him laugh, "You're crazy lady, you know that. But too dangerous for me." He is swinging the lasso overhead.

Robert's Story XIV

"Jake, is that you?" My mind reels as I try to remember who I called.

"Yeah, it's me." He is panting loudly. "Can't talk. Running after Simone."

"Hold on, hold on. What do you mean, running after Simone? Where? Why?"

"I'm on an old road in the park and we are heading for, oh, I forget where but Simone is dead set on getting somewhere fast. She threw me her phone when it rang so she didn't have to deal with it. Gotta go. I'm losing her and wherever she is going I want to go too. Something exciting must be going down!"

"No, wait. Wait! Where are you? Have you seen my mother?"

"Heading toward … where are we going Simone? It's Robert."

I hear Simone call out from a distance. "Upper ball fields. Larry is supposed to be there and I need to see Larry."

"Who's Larry?" Jake hollers.

"Trouble."

"Jake, Jake, come back on the phone. Is my mother there?" I scream.

"I hope not, Robert. There's trouble ahead."

The phone goes dead and I peel out of the parking lot, heading to the other side of the park. How did Simone and Jake hook up? Things are all out of kilter.

-43-

Zigzagging

In desperation I abandon the trail and race through the woods in an attempt to get to the gravel access road that runs along the bottom of the steep hill that the fields sit atop. If I get to the road and get a head start, I can round the corner and climb up onto the field area where there are lots of people. I don't hear Larry's cart anymore. Could he have given up? I consider for a minute but know I can't risk it. I fight my way through undergrowth and, with a huge effort, pop up onto the gravel road. I stop and catch my breath. I can't hear him. Maybe he was just trying to scare me. Maybe he's playing rodeo. I start the uphill walk on the gravel way as it slowly winds up to the fields. And there it is again, that horrid mechanical noise. I look back and Larry is surging forward on his vehicle, lasso whirling above his head. He'll catch me in a minute. I'm petrified by the twirling lasso. I run as fast as I can, zigzagging along the road. I don't want to be an easy target. But he is getting closer, so, in desperation, I turn left and address the vertical hill that rises before me. It's a short-cut up to the ball fields if one can make the climb. With determination and much difficulty, I begin to scale the steep embankment. I grab onto tree trunks and scramble on all fours. Near the top, my feet slip and I reach out to stop myself falling. I spy something jutting from the wall. I latch on and find myself hanging over the hillside. I look up and see I am dangling by a couple of roots that curve in and out of the dirt. I want to cry out but, as I look down, I see Larry has just turned the bend in the road and will soon be below me. If I fall it will be right into his vehicle … and rope. I pedal my feet and somehow, gain purchase. I make the final scramble to the top and plop myself onto level ground.

Robert's Story XV

As I enter the parking lot I get stuck in a line of cars. There's a game in progress but more children are showing up. C'mon. C'mon! A car in front of me stops to unload two kids with mitts and a bag of baseballs. One drops his glove and the other, a wiseguy, kicks it out of reach. They look at each other and giggle before the boy picks up his glove. Could they move any slower? Finally I get to a parking spot, but not before bumping over a discarded baseball bat. I jump out of the car. Looking through the crowd of parents and kids in uniforms, I don't see Simone or Jake. They'd stand out here, I think. No sign of Mom either. That could be good or bad. I scan the area again, and there, behind the bleachers at the edge of the field, I see someone flop over the rim of the hillside. I squint. It can't be, I think. As I move through little leaguers, I hear something out of place. I turn, and there is a small vehicle rising over the edge of the hillside to the left. The man on the cart seems to be swinging something. He looks out of place, menacing really. I look back to the person getting to their feet on my far right. Mom! As I start over, yelling her name, someone catches my sleeve. It's Jake.

~44~

Chain link fence

I look around. Relief floods through me. I am at the edge of the ballpark behind a small section of chain link fence. People are gathered for a game. Boys are dotting the field in front of me, each bent over, ready to field the ball. The pitcher is winding up and a small boy is standing in front of the home plate umpire, bat over his shoulder. And then, suddenly, the noise again. Larry! Turning, I see him round the side of the slope at the end of the field area. The serenity of the children playing baseball against a crazy man on a small garden vehicle swinging a lasso panics me.

I whirl around. How can I be among so many people and yet no one sees what is happening? The dreadful sound of the motor is louder and I look up to see Larry barreling toward me, skirting the people milling around the edge of the field. I cry out, waving my hands, but the cheering for the teams overpowers my voice. Everyone's back is to me because they are watching a game. I look across the field at the kids on alert as the ball is pitched. Larry is so close I can almost feel the wind from his lasso. Seeing no other option, I run around the fence and onto the baseball diamond.

Robert's Story XVI

"Jake!" I yell in relief. "What's going on?"

"Not sure. I lost Simone. Did you see her... Whoa, police cars."

I turn to look behind me and sure enough there are black and whites coming one after the other. As I turn back to Jake I am distracted by something that stops me dead. Mom is on the field and that guy in the cart with the rope is coming at her from right field. I grab Jake's arm.

~45~

Ineligible older player on field

I find myself in the middle of the game just as a ball careens between first and second. I leap in the air, avoiding the ball, and round second just behind the little leaguer. Behind me, I can sense Larry is on the field too as the parents start screaming. The home plate umpire is yelling and waving his arms as I run toward the base. At that moment, the player in front of me slides into third. The fielder has the ball in his glove and is lunging toward the runner's feet. They meet at the bag. I stop to avoid colliding with them. I look down and they look up at me in anticipation. I stare back at Larry who has the home plate umpire on the ground with a lasso around his chest protector. I look back at the kids, their faces anxious for the call. "Safe," I yell, splaying my arms widely.

Then I see fathers pouring out of the stands onto the field. I pivot my head around, wondering where to go next. The field is full of kids and parents. And in the distance, I see police cars pulling into the lot. And Simone is waving at them to come to the field – where did she come from? Is that Jake standing behind her? I look back at the field. Dads are grabbing kids and some are chasing Larry. Is one of them Robert? I think I'm going crazy.

I twirl around, looking in all directions. I feel disoriented by the surging people and the presence of Simone, Robert, and Jake. I lurch forward and stumble into left field hitting my head rather hard on the grassy outfield. As I drift into a stupor thoughts keep rounding in my head – impersonating an umpire, rounding second without running the first base line, ineligible older player on the field.

-46-

Deafening quiet

When I come to, I am alone on the field. Larry is backed up to the concession stand and is surrounded by a semicircle of police including Simone. Jake and Robert are in this group as well. Behind them is a row of angry parents. I stagger over, almost afraid to get near Larry even though he is hemmed in by police. Robert sees me and runs over and hugs me. I hear Simone.

"...charged with the death of Derek Remy". As she launches into his rights, Larry starts to yell "No. No. No" and tries to get away. I involuntarily step back.

"I didn't do it," Larry cries defiantly. "I was goofing around and lassoed him but that was all. He stumbled but I didn't mean anything. Let me go! Leave me alone!"

"And then you hit him, didn't you? You gave him the blow to the head that killed him."

"No, I didn't. You're wrong. Let me go. It wasn't me. I was just playing with the rope, taunting him like my... like she said I should."

"Who is 'she'? Don't make stuff up." Simone continues her charge.

"It was my mother!" Larry yells loudly. Then, more quietly and with control he says, "It was my mother! She did it!" And at that, Larry stares at the ground, hands in fists.

A deafening quiet clouds the field. Even the angry fathers still. Simone pauses, her mouth ajar. "Your mother! Your mother? Who is your mother and what does she have to do with anything?"

She looks around at me and Robert and Jake as if we have insight. We shrug and shake our heads. Simone grabs Larry by the shirt and pulls him toward her. "Who is your mother?"

Larry looks up at Simone, hate in his eyes. "Margot. Margot is my mother."

-47-

Watching a movie

I sit down hard on the field. Simone is bustling Larry off in an official car. Through a fog, I watch the umpire trying to get the game restarted. I feel groggy. Robert pulls out a water bottle, tilts my head and gives me a sip of water. The coldness of the drink doesn't clear my head.

"Larry." I say. "He had that lasso. How do we know he didn't kill Derek? And Margot?" I shake my head. "I never liked her."

"We'll have to wait and see. Simone will wrap it all up."

I start to ramble, scenarios popping into my head. "So the developers hired Larry to dispose of the body after his mother killed Derek? Or Dale and Larry worked together under Margot's evil guidance. I mean Larry is the one with a lasso and seems to know how to use it. Oh, we'll never sort this out." I rub my forehead.

"Simone will explain when she sorts it out. I'm going to take you home."

"But my car is..."

"It'll keep. We'll get it later."

"But wait a minute. How did you know to come to these fields?"

"Simone asked John Logan where Larry was and he said Larry was heading to the fields. Then Simone ran into Jake on the trail and he asked her how to get back to his car which was parked in the upper lots so she told him, and seeing she was running for all she was worth, he took off after her to see what was up. I spoke to Jake and he gave me the short version while he was running. I was already in the Administrative lot – I followed you after you left the bistro – so then I made a quick exit and came over here just as you were coming up the embankment. Then Larry buzzed up and, well, it was quite a fourth inning."

"But how did you get here so fast? I thought you were interviewing..."

"I blew that off. Like I said. I came here because I realized I needed to follow you."

"So Simone was after Larry?"

"Don't worry about it. Let's get home. But you were right to have a fascination with the crazy park employees. You had a sense about them. And I don't think Dale was involved. Or the developers."

I follow Robert to his car. Jake jumps in the back. "Glad to see you're okay," he says, patting my shoulder from the back seat. "It was like watching a movie, you out there running from a felon. You umping a little league game at the same time. Really, someone needs to write this down."

-48-

Wild run

It's a few days later. My head is clear, no concussion. Robert and Simone are relieved. They really didn't want me to join their TBI club. And Sarah Jane is resting upstairs. She's going to heal at my house until she is ready to travel. We had quite the discussion about my baseball game heroics. Mostly I had to explain baseball to her so she could understand what happened on the field. She was demanding for details. I haven't spoken with Simone. I know Larry accused his mother. And that his mother was Margot. That explains the wrangling I heard from the office. The thing is, why did she do it? What was her problem with Derek?

I sit and ponder these questions, questions I have posed at the restaurant to Robert and Jake to no avail. Then I hear Simone's car pop up the driveway. I dash to the door.

"What's up?" I ask. "Any news on the case?"

"Yep," she says. "You broke it wide open with your wild run through the infield."

"How?"

"Actually, that's not really true. I just had to comment on that passion play. I had determined it was Larry – remember when I met you on my way into the Administration Building? Well, when we did our fingerprinting and it came up that Larry was not Larry Cloud at all. His real name is Lou Caccio. And, thanks to Larry's outburst, we now know that Margot is Mary Caccio."

"What about John Logan? He must be part of that mess."

"John Logan is Margot's, er, Mary's, brother. She has something on him. Not sure what yet, but she made him hire Larry, er, Lou."

"Stick with the names I know. Move along."

"OK, well Larry is AWOL from the Army and it appears Derek discovered this. Not sure why he was poking around the DOD site of AWOL soldiers, but we know he was because… well, I'll explain that later. Anyway, there was Margot, happily hiding her son Larry in Rob Ryan Park, through some threat to her brother John – real name by the way. And then Derek ran into Margot and Larry near the pavilion and he let them know that he knew about Larry. Said he was turning him in. So, at Margot's insistence Larry grabbed the rope on his utility vehicle and lassoed Derek as he turned his back to him. Derek fell to the ground and Margot grabbed a large piece of firewood and killed Derek. Then she drafted her brother into the horrific plan to bury Derek in the park. Margot wasn't going to confess to anything but Larry was so angry, that she finally confessed to the whole story. John won't admit to anything. Says he knew nothing and had nothing to do with burying a body. No one believes that but we're still working on how Margot convinced him to hire her and Larry. Anyway, John's most definitely gone from park employment, taking his pencils with him. Did you ever see those pencils he keeps in a line on his desk? When I first saw those pointy things I thought, 'This man is tightly screwed and is trying to hold onto his sanity.'"

"They fascinated me too! I just wanted to roll them onto the floor and see his reaction." I pause and look intently at Simone. "So when I found the hand, they were scared, weren't they?"

"Yep. And Larry and Margot were against John even reporting the hand in the wall. But I guess he figured you wouldn't let it go. Congratulations, you were a pain in the ass to all three."

"Oh, I'm good at that. And Larry's fascination with camo. He was playing soldier."

"Apparently that suited him more than being a soldier. I don't think Larry ever quite grew up. He liked to play soldier so his mother thought, sign him up. And we know how that worked out. So she covered for him and found a place for the two of them to disappear. She was the puppet master. In fact, behind that counter of hers we found all kind of interesting things. Complaints about Larry's behavior in the park, hikers saying someone came out of the woods and scared them, people saying he was driving the cart in a menacing way, an incident where he was dragging himself along the ground holding a big stick as a gun. All buried in Margot's papers. She stood behind that desk and manipulated John and the public."

"Wow. And Margot told you Derek approached Larry about being AWOL?"

"Yes, she and Larry. And, get this, Derek's missing laptop was tucked under Margot's counter."

"I knew there was something weird there. And I knew they didn't like me. What about Sarah Jane? Did Larry push her?"

"Not sure we'll ever know that. Although, I do have a question for you. Don't know if you'll be able to answer it but... Why do you think Larry suddenly went after you with such a vengeance? I know he'd been harassing you in the woods a bit and possibly had a hand in Sarah Jane's fall, but it seemed like suddenly he came after you out of nowhere."

"Well, he was on Bunny Hill with me and he was driving that vehicle of his and giving me a dirty look and then... Oh boy. Oh boy! I had just found out that he was the same guy that wore the camo and, so I said to him 'you're two people' meaning I thought he was two different people – the camo guy and the maintenance guy – but, oh, he thought I meant something else."

"He thought you knew his secret!"

~49~

Classic books

So Dale did buy that farm. And Dale did give Chloe her money for the school. I saw both of them at the bistro opening a couple of weeks ago and they've developed a close professional relationship to support the school. Dale is even reading classic books now.

And the Bistro opened and is a hit. Reservations are soaring and with Christmas coming, the gang are hoping to really cash in. I'm afraid I may be roped into waiting tables or washing dishes, but I have always said if they need anything...

I arrive home late one evening to find Terence in my kitchen with Sarah Jane.

"What's up?" I say.

Terence looks at me. "I returned your chiminea."

He points out the window and there sit Sebastian, Bobby, and Robert with fancy drinks in their hands. The grill is smoking.

"Thanks, Terence. Good man. But why did you steal it and why did you pick on my street, Summer Street?"

"Well, one night, early days in the restaurant planning, Bobby and Sebastian and Robert walked over to your place to cook some steaks and sit by the chiminea. I heard Robert say that you were out and they could hang out on the patio and he could fire up the grill. Sebastian grabbed a bottle and as they started out the door, I followed. But Bobby told me I had to stay behind to do some dumb ass job. The cookout was for owners only. He was always treating me like I didn't count for crap. So I asked Robert where your house was and he said, '321 Summer Street'. Bobby turned around, pointed at me and said, 'Don't be showing up. Lock up when you're done.' So, I kind of had a grudge. And, I took it out on the wrong people."

"Ah. They weren't nice to you. You know you're welcome here anytime. Tell Bobby I said that."

I look at Sarah Jane and then back at Terence. "What are you and Sarah Jane up to?"

"I'm making a Victoria Sponge under Sarah Jane's guidance. A replacement if you will. And I put back the red shoes and golf clubs and bought a plant for the neighbors down the street and I am slowly paying off the alcohol I lifted. And Robert sat Bobby and I down and we had a 'session.'"

I smile. "How do you like baking?"

"He has a knack I think," says Sarah Jane, jumping in like a proud mother. "I'm trying to talk him into culinary school. We're going to bake everyday for the next week and I'll see if I can interest him."

"I heard from someone that Bistro on High needs desserts," I add.

~50~

A stick figure

Later, when I am alone, I walk into the dining room and look at the Crime Board. After considering for a minute, I head up to my computer to find photos. Sure enough, Margot's and Larry's pictures are in the paper. I print them out. I go back downstairs to the Crime Board and add the three from the park. Larry's goes up, his name changes to Larry Cloud nee Lou Caccio. And likewise, Margot is now, gee, I never knew her assumed last name. She is now Margot nee Mary Caccio. I represent John Logan as a stick figure. He sort of was a stick figure in real life, I muse. Stiff, supporting his sister at his own risk, no personality.

But the sad thing is that Derek's life was ended at the hands of this unsavory trio.

I sit down at the table to think. I never knew Derek and yet I sort of mourn him. I never knew Rhonda but I feel badly about her death as well. But, trying to find good in the bad, I think about the new people in my life. I now know Sarah Jane and Dale. Terence spends a lot of time in my kitchen. And Jake and I have formed a bond as well. I think I'll give him a bag of walnuts for Christmas.

The End

42141774R00137